TREASURE ISLAND

According to

SPIKE MILLIGAN

This paperback edition first published in 2001 by
Virgin Books Ltd
Thames Wharf Studios
Rainville Road
London
W6 9HA

First published in Great Britain in 2000 by Virgin Publishing Ltd

Reprinted 2003

A catalogue record for this book is available from the British Library.

ISBN 0 7535 0503 7

Typeset by TW Typesetting, Plymouth, Devon
Printed and bound in Great Britain by
Mackays of Chatham PLC

TREASURE ISLAND

According to
SPIKE MILLIGAN

Prologue
How Groucho joined the crew

Q: Are you, Groucho Marx, willing to appear in 'TREASURE ISLAND'?

Groucho: Oh? What's in it for me, my good man?

Q: Fame and fortune!

Groucho: Never mind that, what about the money?

Q: Who's talking about money?

Groucho: No one. That's why I mentioned it.

Q: In this book no one gets paid.

Groucho: Well, I wish them luck and goodbye, suckers.

Q: Wait! In your case perhaps we can come to some special arrangement.

Groucho: In my case, my special arrangement is money.

Q: What do you want?

Groucho: Ten dollars a word.

Q: What if you don't speak?

Groucho: Then I'll get fuck all.

Q: Supposing we paid a dollar a word?

Groucho: Then I'd talk very fast.

Q: OK, you're on, a dollar a word.

Groucho: I agree. Yes I agree, yes I agree, I agree. That'll be sixty two dollars.

Q: Have you change for a hundred?

Groucho: No, but I'll keep it till I do.

Q: Right, sign this agreement.

Groucho: I'll just sign it with a cross.

Q: A cross? Are you illiterate?

Groucho: Heavens no. I can spell cross.

Q: You are a difficult man to deal with.

Groucho: Sometimes if the date is right, I'm a difficult woman to deal with.

Bow! Wow! Wow!

Groucho: Whose dog is that?

PART ONE

Captain Flint

The Old Sea Dog At The 'Admiral Benbow'

1

I remember him as if it were yesterday. As a matter of fact it *was* yesterday. He came plodding to the inn door. I distinctly heard him going plod-plod-plod; a tall, strong, heavy, nut-brown man. He was an unforgettable sight: his tarry pigtail falling over the shoulders of his shit-covered blue coat; his hands with black, broken nails; and the sabre-cut across one cheek a dirty, livid white. I remember him looking round the cove and whistling to himself. As he did so he broke out into the most boring old sea song that was not in the charts at the time:

> *Fifteen men on the dead man's chest –*
> *Yo-ho-ho, and a bottle of rum!*

It was an old tottering voice, so tottering I thought it was going to fall off. Then he rapped on the door with something that looked like a handspike. On inspection it proved to be something that looked like a handspike. When my father appeared, the man called roughly for a glass of rum.

'You! I roughly want a glass of rum!'

'There,' said my father setting it down, 'that's roughly a glass of rum.'

This he drank slowly like a connoisseur, lingering on the taste tho' he knew bugger all about rum.

'This is a handy cove,' said he at length, five feet eleven inches. 'Much company, mate?'

My father told him we weren't a company, we relied on a few Japanese tourists but as there was no golf course, they left.

'Well, then,' said he, 'this is the berth for me. Here you, matey,' he cried to a cripple who trundled the barrow. 'Bring up alongside and help up with my chest.'

So he helped him up with his chest which when expanded was forty-two inches.

'I'm a plain man; rum bum baccy, and bacon and eggs is what I want. You mought call me captain. Oh? I see what you're at – there.' He threw down three or four gold pieces on the floor. My father snatched them up and swallowed them for safety. 'You can tell me when I've worked through that.'

Groucho: You look like a seasoned rum bum and baccy old sailor.

Captain: Aye, seasoned with rum bum baccy and women.

Groucho: I wish you luck with all of them. You certainly have a wide choice. What did you do on your shore leave?

Captain: I think she was called Deptford Flo; coo, she was hot stuff.

Groucho: Hot stuff? Did she burn you?

Captain: No, no. Just beware of women.

Groucho: My mother's a woman, she does B&B.

Captain: B&B?

Groucho: Yes, B&B, breakfast and bugger off.

Captain: Ah, breakfast and bugger off!
Mothers are a wonderful thing.
Groucho: Was Deptford Flo a mother?
Captain: Frequently.
Groucho: Who was the father?
Captain: The crew of *HMS Ironsides*.

My mother called me over. She said, 'Jim, I want you to keep away from that man. He's a bad influence. He's vulgar and he smells.'

'I know but you soon get used to it.'

I went down to the cellar and adjusted all the bungs on the beer barrels, but I couldn't get the Captain out of my mind. He was a rough, rude, rum bum and baccy sailor. He kept letting off; then you had to stand clear.

The next morning I served him his breakfast of rum bum baccy, egg and bacon.

Captain: Ah, fit for a king, my boy.
Jim: You know, Captain, the Jews are not supposed to eat bacon.
Captain: Thank God I'm not a Jew, Jim.
Jim: What are you, Captain?
Groucho: I'll tell you, he's methylated spirits.
Jim: Oh? Methylated spirits? What's that?
Groucho: Yes, I'd like to know what that is too.
Jim: Captain, tell me about some of your sea battles.
Captain: Oh, Jim, there was a time we boarded a Spanish galleon. I was set upon by a huge Spaniard.

Jim: Oh, did he hurt you?

Captain: No, I shot him before he could. I threw him over the side. He said, 'Señor, I can't swim.' I said, 'Look, I can't play the violin but I don't shout about it!'

My mother, who had been watching, shouted, 'Jim, come away from that man.'

'But, Mum, he's not doing me any harm,' I said.

'Come away before you feel the back of my hand!'

So I came away and felt the back of her hand. It was like playing a flesh-covered piano.

The Captain was a very silent man by custom. All day he hung around the cove with a brass telescope singing:

Fifteen men on the dead man's chest —
Etc., etc., etc.

Groucho: I've never heard a brass telescope singing before. There must be a first for everything.

Mostly he would not speak when spoken to; so he did not ever speak. Every day, when he came back from his stroll, he would ask if any seafaring men had been. When a seaman put up at the 'Admiral Benbow' he would look at him through the crack in his trousers. He promised me a silver fourpenny on the first of every month if I would keep my 'weather-eye open for a seafaring man with one leg'. I didn't have any weather-eyes so I never saw a seafaring man with one leg.

But how that personage haunted my dreams. Now the leg would be cut off at the knee, now at the hip, now at the shoulders, then the neck; now he was a monstrous kind of a creature. I would dream of him chasing me on his one leg joined to his neck.

Though I was terrified by the idea of the seafaring man with one leg, I was less afraid of the Captain himself . . . but then he had *two* legs. There were nights when he took a great deal more rum and water than his head would carry; then he would sit and sing his number one in the charts; Madonna was a close second:

Fifteen men on the dead man's chest –
Etc., etc., etc.

Sometimes he would call for glasses all round, and force all the trembling company to sing: 'Sing, you buggers, sing.'

Often I have heard the house shaking with 'Yo-ho-ho, and a bottle of rum, etc., etc.,' all the neighbours joining in for dear life, with the fear of death upon them, each singing louder than the other. He could fly up in a passion of anger when asked Why did a chicken cross the road?

Groucho: To get to the other seed or to see Gregory Peck.

His stories were what frightened people worst of all. Dreadful stories they were; about hanging, walking the plank, swallowing the anchor, and the Clap. He must have mixed among some of the wickedest men that God ever allowed like Charlie Chester, Chris Evans and Terry Wogan.

TREASURE ISLAND

My father was always saying, 'the Inn will be ruined,' he was always saying, 'the Inn will be ruined,' 'the Inn will be ruined . . .'

Jim: Don't worry, dad, the Inn is doing good business.

Father: Not really, son, the Captain hasn't paid any rent for weeks.

Jim: I suppose he hasn't got it.

Father: Well if he hasn't got it the Inn will be ruined. The rent is two weeks overdue and your mother is five weeks overdue. I tell you the Inn will be ruined.

Jim: Dad, we took four pounds ten shillings at the bar last night.

Father: Yes, but I still say the Inn will be ruined . . . I don't feel well, Jim.

So I felt him all over and sure enough he didn't feel well all over. 'Why don't you go to bed?'

Mother tucked him in with a hot water bottle. 'I think you should see a doctor,' she said, and Dad said, 'Shouldn't he see me? I think it's an attack of malaria; I got it when I was serving in India.'

Mother: Why in God's name did you bring it back here?

Father: It travelled with me.

Bow wow! Bow wow!

Groucho: Whose dog is that?

We thought that the Captain would eventually tyrannise the people and soon they would cease coming but I really believe his presence did us good. There was even

11

a party of young men and women who would admire him, calling him a 'true sea-dog', and a 'sea cat', even a 'sea hamster', saying that he was the sort of man that made England terrible at sea and just as terrible on land.

He kept staying on week after week; at last month after month so that all the money had long been exhausted, and still my father never plucked up the heart to insist on having more rent. If ever he mentioned it, the Captain would roar and stare my father out of the room. I am sure the terror my father lived in must have greatly hastened his early death.

All the time he lived with us the Captain did nothing. He did the lottery, of course, but apart from that, nothing. He didn't even wash. When he was up on the cliff a mile away we could still smell him down at the inn. In his room he kept a great sea-chest none of us had ever seen open. He'd stand on it and cross himself. Why not? He had crossed everybody else. Towards the end, when my poor father was far gone into decline and lay on his deathbed, Dr Livesey came late one afternoon to see the patient.

Groucho: Doctor, where did you study medicine?
Doctor: St John's College.
Groucho: A medical school?
Doctor: No, it was a college for farmers. I realised that when they asked me how to milk a cow.
Groucho: So what is your hobby, doctor?
Doctor: I like milking cows.

Groucho: Isn't that boring?

Doctor: Only after three churns.

Groucho: That's a lot of milk. What did you do with it?

Doctor: Oh, I poured it back into the cow.

Groucho: Didn't that make them leak?

Doctor: Yes, but when you couldn't see where they were, you could certainly see where they'd been.

I remember observing the contrast: the neat, bright doctor, with his powder-wig as white as snow, and his bright, black eyes and pleasant manner, compared with that filthy, shit-strewn, bearded scarecrow of a pirate of ours, sitting far gone in rum, with his arms on the table. Suddenly he – the Captain, that is – began to sing in the charts again:

Fifteen men on the dead man's chest –
Etc., etc., etc.

The doctor said to my father, 'Now, Mr Hawkins, let's have a look at you.'

'Will that make him better?' asked mother.

'He's got a temperature,' said the doctor. 'Make him drink lots of water. If he won't drink it, throw it over him.'

At first I had supposed 'the dead man's chest' to be that identical big box of the Captain's upstairs in the front room, and the thought had been mingled in my nightmares with that of the one-legged seafaring man. The Captain suddenly smashed his hand upon the table; the table and his hand fell to bits. We knew that to mean

– silence. Dr Livesey, the idiot, went on talking as before. The Captain glared at him. 'Silence, you bastard.'

'Were you addressing me, sir?' says the silly doctor; and the ruffian had told him, with another oath, 'fuck', that this was so. 'I have only one thing to say to you, sir,' replied the doctor. 'Keep on drinking rum, and the world will soon be quit of a very dirty scoundrel – you'll snuff it!'

'Bollocks!' he said. He sprang to his feet, drew and opened a sailor's clasp-knife.

The doctor never moved. He spoke to him over his shoulder, it nearly broke his neck. The same tone of voice, rather high as if he were queer:

'If you do not put that knife away, sailor, I promise you shall be put in stocks.'

'Fuck the stocks,' said the Captain.

'I will not fuck the stocks,' said the doctor. 'And now, sir, I will have you know I am a magistrate and if I catch a breath of complaint against you, I'll revolve your swonnicles and after a fair trial you will be hung.'

'Get fucked,' said the sailor.

Soon Dr Livesey's horse came to the door and he rode away to get fucked, leaving my father in his deathbed. 'We will be ruined,' he said, 'you'll see.'

So we waited to see us all ruined.

Groucho: So far, so good, that'll be $171, please.

Bow wow! Bow wow!

Groucho: Whose dog *is* that?

Black Dog Appears And Disappears

2

It was plain from the first that my father was little likely to see the spring. He sank down daily and my mother had to pull him out. Mother and I had all the inn in our hands as my father lay dying. Mother took up sleep walking. Why she didn't waken as she clumped out of the inn in her walking boots, I'll never know. Still, it was good healthy exercise for her.

Jim:	Mum, where was Dad born?
Mum:	In Bexhill-on-Sea.
Jim:	Where is that?
Mum:	That's a village for the dying by the sea.
Jim:	Was he dying?
Mum:	No, he managed to escape before he did.
Jim:	How did he escape?
Mum:	He jumped out of his coffin and ran.
Jim:	What was he doing in a coffin?
Mum:	He was waiting to die.
Jim:	What was he dying of?
Mum:	Lurgy.
Jim:	What's that?
Mum:	Like spots of shit on the liver.

Jim:	Is that dangerous?
Mum:	Only if you've got it.
Jim:	How do you cure it?
Mum:	You jump out of your coffin and run away.
Jim:	How do you catch it?
Mum:	By living at Bexhill-on-Sea.

The Captain had risen earlier and higher than usual and so set out for the beach as though his mind was still on Dr Livesey who was away getting fucked.

My mother was downstairs while my father lay upstairs dying. When the parlour door opened and a man stepped in, I asked him what he wanted. 'What do you want?' I said. He said he would take some rum. As I was going out of the room to fetch it he went to sit down upon a table, missed it, then motioned me to draw near with the rum.

'Come here, sonny,' says he.

'Is this here table for my mate Bill?' he asked.

I told him I did not know his mate Bill; and this was for a person who stayed in our house, whom we called the Captain.

'Ah,' said he, 'that'll be my rum bum and baccy mate Bill called the Captain, as like as not.'

'Yes and his rent is three months overdue. Would you like to pay it?'

The man fainted.

I told him the Captain was out walking in the London Marathon.

Groucho: Ah, what a disguise.

The stranger hung about outside the inn door waiting for the Marathon to finish. My mother went upstairs to watch my father lying dying for a while.

'Aarh, sure enough,' he said, 'here comes my mate Bill, with a spy-glass under his arm.'

So saying, the stranger backed along with me into the parlour. He cleared the hilt of his cutlass and loosened the blade in the sheath. Was he going to kill him? All the time we were waiting he kept swallowing, as if he felt what we used to call a lump in the throat. He didn't know it was cancer.

At last the Captain ran in from the Marathon. He had been placed 74th out of a field of 22. He marched straight across the room to where his rum bum and baccy breakfast awaited him.

'Bill,' said the stranger, in a voice he was trying to make bold and big.

The Captain spun round and round and round and round. When he stopped revolving he was face-to-face with the stranger, a nasty shock for both of them.

'Come, Bill, you know me,' said the stranger.

The Captain made a sort of gasp in his voice. 'Black Dog!' said he with a sort of gasp in his voice.

Bow wow! Bow wow!

Groucho: Is that you, Black Dog?

'And who else?' returned the other, getting more at his ease. 'Black Dog as ever was, coming for to see his old shipmate Billy.'

Groucho: Black Dog? Isn't that what
Churchill suffered from?

'Now, look here,' said the Captain; 'you've run me down; speak up: what is it?'

'That's you, Bill,' returned Black Dog, 'I'll have a glass of rum. We'll sit down, if you please, and talk square, like old shipmates.'

So they talked square like old shipmates.

When I returned with the rum Black Dog was next to the door so as to have one eye on his old shipmate, and one on his retreat.

I left them together and retired to the bar. I heard nothing, I listened intently; sure enough I heard low gabbling; but at last the voices began to grow higher and higher till they were about three feet above ground level, and I could pick up a word or two, 'fish' and 'bite'.

'No, no, no, no!' cried the Captain. 'If it comes to swinging, swing all, say I.'

Suddenly there was a tremendous noise – a clash of steel followed, and then a cry of pain, 'Ahgggggggah!' In the next instant Black Dog was in full flight, the Captain hotly pursuing.

'I'll have your balls for trophies!' shouted the Captain, streaming blood from the left shoulder. The Captain aimed at the fugitive one last tremendous cut, and missed.

Once out upon the road, Black Dog showed a clean pair of heels. The Captain stood staring after him.

'Jim,' says he, 'rum;' and as he spoke, he reeled a little, and steadied himself with one hand against the wall.

'Are you hurt?' cried I.

'Are you bloody blind?' he said.

'No, I'm not blind,' I said.

19

'Rum,' he repeated. 'I must get away from here. Rum bum and baccy!'

So I ran to fetch him his rum bum and baccy. I heard a loud fall in the parlour and, running in, beheld the Captain lying face down, full length, five feet eleven inches, upon the floor. At the same instant my mother, alarmed by the cries and fighting, came running downstairs while my father lay upstairs dying on his deathbed. Between us we raised the Captain's head and left his body where it was. The Captain was breathing loud and hard. His eyes, mouth and teeth were open for business, his face a horrible colour – magenta.

'Dear, deary me,' cried my mother, 'what a horrible colour – it doesn't match the curtains!'

We had no idea what to do for the Captain. I tried to pour some rum down his throat but his teeth were now tightly shut so with an enema we squirted it up his bottom.

Doctor Livesey came in to visit my father who lay dying.

'Oh Doctor,' we cried, 'what shall we do? Where is he wounded?'

'Wounded? Fiddle-sticks. The man has had a stroke, a stroke of luck for his wife, she has his life policy. Now, Mrs Hawkins, just you run upstairs to your husband, and tell him, if possible, nothing about it.'

So she ran upstairs and, if possible, said nothing about it.

'Jim, get me a basin.'

When I got back with the basin, the doctor had already ripped up the Captain's sleeve, and exposed his great sinewy arm. It was tattooed in several places.

'Here's luck', 'A fair wind', and his National Lottery numbers.

'Now, Jim, we will have a look at the colour of his blood. It should be red. Are you afraid of blood, Jim?'

'No, sir,' said I. 'I'm full of it.'

'Then hold the basin.'

A great deal of Blood Group G was taken before the Captain opened his eyes. He recognised the doctor with an unmistakable frown.

'That will be ten shillings,' said the doctor.

The Captain fainted. Suddenly his colour changed, puce, and he tried to raise himself, crying:

'Where's Black Dog?'

'There is no Black Dog here, he's buggered off and you have had a stroke, and I, very much against my own will, dragged you head-foremost out of the grave. Now Mr Bones –'

'That's not my name,' he interruped, 'it's my *nom de plume*.'

'Man, what I have to say is one glass of rum won't kill you but if you take another, you'll die or at least try to. This once I'll help you to your bed.' And for once he helped the Captain to his bed.

We managed to hoist him upstairs, and laid him on his bed, where his head fell back on the pillow, as if he were almost fainting. My father was still lying dying on his deathbed.

'Now, mind you,' said the doctor, 'the name of rum is death.'

Groucho: It'll never catch on. Who'd buy booze labelled 'DEATH'?

'This is nothing,' he said. 'I have drawn blood enough to keep him quiet a while; he should lie for a week where he is – that is the best thing for him and you; but another stroke would kill him.'

Groucho: Lucky he's not a pussy cat.

And with that he went off to see my father, who lay dying on his deathbed.

Groucho: Look, I don't like being in the same room as this lunatic Captain. He might decide he needs to use *my* blood.
Jim: You're speaking of a dying man.
Groucho: Dying? That's the last thing a man should do.

The Black Spot

3

About noon I stopped at the Captain's door with some cooling drinks and medicines and I threw them over him.

'Jim,' he said, 'bring me a noggin of rum.'

'Remember what the doctor said,' I warned him. ' "The name of rum is death." '

'Fuck the doctor,' he said. 'Doctors is all swabs,' he said; 'and that doctor there, why, what do he know about seafaring men? I been in places hot as pitch, and mates dropping all round with Yellow Jack, and with decks awash with dysentery.'

'No,' I said, 'you are not to have your rum bum and baccy now.'

'Oh, my blood'll be on you.'

Groucho: Jim, it will never wash out.

'Look, Jim,' he said, 'how my fingers fidget.'
I watched his fingers fidget.

Groucho: Some people will watch anything for entertainment.

'I can't keep them still; they will go on fidgeting as long as I don't get rum.'

So to stop his fingers fidgeting, I got him some rum.

'If I don't get some rum I will have the horrors.'

'We don't have horrors, we only have eggs and bacon.'

'I seen old Flint,' he said, 'and if I get the horrors and eggs and bacon I will raise Cain.'

'You can't,' I said, 'he's been dead about three thousand years.'

'Oh,' said the Captain, 'I only just heard about it. I'll give you a golden guinea for a noggin, Jim.'

Jim:	Why do you drink it?
Captain:	It gets me there.
Jim:	Where is there?
Captain:	Here.
Jim:	Here? But you're always here.
Captain:	Yes. See? It works!
Jim:	It doesn't take you somewhere else.
Captain:	This is somewhere else.
Jim:	Were you Flint's cabin boy?
Captain:	Yes. One morning I said, 'I've brought your breakfast up.' He said, 'Serves you right for eating it. Ha, ha.'
Jim:	Was he cruel?
Captain:	If you misbehaved he'd bury you up to your neck in shit.
Jim:	Did he shoot anyone?
Captain:	Yes. He shot the ship's cat every day until it ran out of lives.
Jim:	Did he make many enemies?
Captain:	He didn't make 'em; they was already there.
Jim:	Did you battle with the French?

Captain:	Oh, yes I did; I threatened a French sailor with my cutlass. He jumped overboard, he started to drown. 'Help, help,' he shouted, 'I can't swim.' 'Look,' I said, 'I can't play the fiddle but I don't shout about it.'
Jim:	What was your happiest moment?
Captain:	Ah! I can't remember her name.
Jim:	Have you shot anybody?
Captain:	Yes, anybody!
Jim:	What was your mother's name?
Captain:	Richard, she was a man.
Jim:	How did he give birth to you?
Captain:	With great difficulty.

'I want none of your money, Captain,' said I, 'but what you owe my father who is upstairs dying on his deathbed. I'll get you one glass, and no more.'

When I brought it to him, he seized it greedily, and drank. It ran out the other end.

'Ah, ay,' said he, 'that's some better. And now, matey, did that doctor say how long I was to lie here in this old berth?'

'At least a week,' I said.

'A week! I can't do that: they'd have the black spot on me by then.'

'What is a black spot? Is it an accident?'

Grasping my shoulder he struggled until he got into a sitting position, and then fell back again.

'That doctor's done me. Jim,' he said at length, five feet eleven inches, 'you saw that seafaring man today?'

'Black Dog?' I asked.

Bow wow! Bow wow!

Groucho: Is that Black Dog?

'Now, if I can't get away they will tip me the black spot. Mind you, it's my old sea-chest they're after. That and this 'ere treasure map.'

He produced an oilskin packet. It contained a tattered old map which he carefully unfolded. It was alarmingly brittle and encrusted with sea salt, sand, seagull shit and bits of Jaffa Cake. Someone had marked an 'X' where the treasure lay. The seagull had marked most everything else.

'But what is the black spot, Captain?' I asked.

'That's a summons, mate. It means your time is up.'

'When is your time up?' I said.

Groucho: I'd say any minute now!

'But keep your weather-eye open, Jim.'

But as things fell out, my poor father, who still lay dying upstairs on his deathbed, died.

The Captain got downstairs next morning on a stretcher. He had his rum bum baccy, eggs and bacon. The night before the funeral of my father who now lay dead on his deathbed upstairs, the Captain was as drunk as ever; it was shocking in a house of mourning to hear him singing:

All the nice girls like a candle,
All the nice girls like a wick.

He was breathing hard and fast, like a man on a steep mountain. When he was drunk he had an alarming way of drawing his cutlass and he swung it around his head taking one of his ears off. Once he cut off the arm of an innocent bystander.

So things passed until the day of the funeral of my father who now lay dead in his coffin. I was full of sad thoughts about his coffin which was drawing slowly along the road. Suddenly I saw someone else drawing slowly along the road. He was blind and he tapped with a white stick; he was hunched as if with age or weakness, and wore a huge old tattered sea cloak. You could see his arse through his trousers. He stopped, raising his voice.

'Will some kind friend help a poor blind man who has lost the precious sight of his eyes in the defence of his country? Where or in what part of this country he may now be?'

'You are at the "Admiral Benbow" Inn, Black Hill Cove, my good man,' said I.

'I hear a voice,' said he. 'Will you give me your hand?'

I held out my hand, and the horrible creature gripped it in a moment like a vice.

'Now, boy,' he said, 'take me to the Captain.'

'Sir,' said I, 'I dare not.'

'Oh,' he sneered, 'take me in straight, or I'll crush your balls.'

And he gave them a wrench that made me cry out. 'OOWWWwwww!'

'Sir,' I said, 'he sits with a drawn cutlass, but his pistol is real.'

'Come, now, march,' interrupted he. 'Lead me to him and when in view cry out, "Here's a friend for you, Bill."'

If you don't I'll do this . . .' and with that he did the Highland Fling so terribly that I fainted.

As I opened the parlour door, I cried out, 'Here's a friend for you, Bill.'

The poor Captain raised his eyes, and at one look the rum went out of him and left him staring. The expression on his face was of terror, mortal sickness – malaria, swamp fever, Yellow Jack and mumps.

'Now, Bill, sit where you are,' said the beggar.

The Captain's finger stirred and the blind man heard it. I saw him pass something from the hollow of the hand that held his stick into the palm of the Captain's, which closed upon it instantly.

'That's done,' said the blind man; and with accuracy and nimbleness, skipped out of the parlour and fell on his face in the road. I could hear his stick go tap-tap-tapping into the distance.

The rum started coming out of the Captain, he stood swaying for a moment, and then with a peculiar sound, Gaglipough!, he fell his whole height, five feet eleven inches, face-foremost on the floor. Alas, my dead father didn't know that now lying dead on the floor was the Captain. He had been struck dead by thundering apoplexy. It was a rare disease only caught from kangaroos. Of late I had begun to pity him, but as I saw him dead, I burst into a great flood of tears, and I had to swim for it.

The Sea-Chest

4

I lost no time, of course, in telling my mother all that I knew, while she wasn't sleep-walking. The neighbour-hood, to our ears, seemed haunted by approaching footsteps; and what with the dead body of the Captain on the parlour floor, and the thought of that detestable blind beggar ready to return, there were moments when I jumped out of my skin in terror and then went back into it again. Something must speedily be done. It occurred to us to go forth together and seek help in the neighbouring hamlet. We ran out at once into the gathering evening; all the while the Captain lay dead on the floor.

Bow wow! Bow wow!

Groucho: Whose dog *is* that?

The hamlet lay not many hundred yards away on the other side of the next cove. We were not many minutes on the road, though we sometimes stopped and I laid hold of my mother and harkened. But there was nothing but the low wash of the ripples and the croaking of the crows in the wood, that and the National Lottery on TV.

It was already candle-light when we reached the hamlet, and I shall never forget how much I was cheered to see the yellow shine in doors and windows. 'Three cheers,' I said, 'for the yellow shine in the doors and windows.' You would have thought men would have been ashamed of themselves not to help us. Not one man would return with us to the 'Admiral Benbow' to stand guard. For that matter, anyone who knew of the terrible Captain, it was enough to frighten them to death. In fact, one of them who knew the Captain was so frightened he dropped dead from fright.

'If none of you will accompany us, we will go back the way we came.' All they would do was to give me a loaded pistol, lest we were attacked.

My heart was beating finely when we two set forth in the cold night upon this dangerous venture. We could neither see nor hear anything to decrease our terrors, till, to our huge relief, the door of the 'Admiral Benbow' had closed behind us.

I slipped the bolt at once, and we stood and panted in the dark, alone in the house with the dead Captain's body on the floor.

'Draw down the blind, Jim,' said mother. 'Now we have to get the key of his chest.'

I felt in his pocket; sure enough it wasn't there.

'Perhaps it's round his neck,' said mother. I tore open his shirt and sure enough it wasn't there either. Finally we found it already in the lock. She turned the key. The lock played a little tune, it had been made in Japan.

There was nothing to be seen on the top. We came across a canvas bag that gave forth at a touch the jingle of gold coins. 'Gold!' I said in an excited voice.

'I'll show these rogues that I'm an honest woman.

Hold my bag,' said my mother. And she began to count over the amount of the Captain's score.

We were about half way through when I suddenly heard a sound that brought my heart into my mouth and out onto the floor. I put my hand on her hand. 'What is it?' said mother. 'It's my hand,' I said. I heard the tap-tap-tapping of the blind man's stick. It drew nearer and nearer, then it struck sharp on the inn door. We could hear the handle being turned, rattling the lock, then a long silence. At last the tapping recommenced, and to our joy it drew slowly away.

'Mother,' said I, 'take the whole lot and let's be going.' I was sure the bolted door would bring a hornet's nest about us.

'I'll take what I have,' she said, jumping to her feet.

'And I'll take this to square the account,' said I, picking up the oilskin packet from the sea-chest. The next moment we were groping each other in the fog.

'My dear,' said my mother suddenly, 'take the money and run on. I am going to faint.'

This was certainly the end for both of us, I thought. How I cursed the cowardice of the neighbours; how I blamed my poor mother for her honesty while the Captain was laying dead upon the floor. I managed to drag my mother down to the bank at the roadside, but it was early closing so we couldn't cash the cheque. So there we had to stay – my mother almost entirely exposed, you could see it all, and both of us within earshot of the inn. Thank heaven nobody tried to shoot at our ears!

Groucho: I must be in this story again soon.
Bow wow! Bow wow!
Groucho: It's that dog again – who owns him?

The Last Of The Blind Man

5

I crept along to the inn again. I sheltered my head
behind a bush of broom, or a broom of bush. I saw my
enemies arrive, seven or eight of them, running hard,
their feet beating out of time. It was exactly four-thirty.
One of them was the blind beggar. The others weren't.

'Down with the door!' he cried. 'Down with Saddam!'

They rushed at it and went straight through and out
of the back. The blind man again cried out, his voice
sounding louder and higher, as if he was afire with
eagerness and rage.

'In, in, in!' he shouted, and cursed them for their
delay.

'Bill's dead!'

Yes indeed, the Captain lay dead on the floor. But the
blind man swore at them again for their delay.

'Search him, some of you shirking lubbers, and the
rest of you aloft and get his sea-chest.'

'They've been before us, Pew. Someone's turned the
chest out alow and aloft.'

'Is it there?' roared Pew.

'Is what there?'

'Oh, anything,' said Pew.

'Flint's fist I mean,' he cried.

'There's no Flint's fist up here,' said the man.

'You below there, is anything on Bill?' cried the blind man.

Another man below began to search the Captain's body.

'I'm sorry, Bill's been overhauled . . . and he's running beautifully.'

'It's those people of the inn – it's that boy. I wish I had put his eyes out!' cried the blind man, Pew. 'Scatter, lads, and find that treasure map.'

There followed a great to-do through all our old inn, the pounding of heavy feet in the search of the treasure map. The buccaneers heard the sound of approaching horses. At last a gallant band of men coming to our aid.

'We left it too late, lads,' said one of the cowards.

The men scattered at the approaching horses' hooves, hives and heeves. Pew stood his ground and was trampled to death and lay dead in the ditch while the Captain lay dead on the floor. I hailed the riders.

'Pew is dead,' I said, 'in the ditch and the Captain is dead on the floor.'

Back at the 'Admiral Benbow' the house was in a state of smash; all the furniture had been thrown down in their furious search for the treasure map.

'What were they after?' said Mr Dance, one of the horsemen.

'Well to tell you the truth, I should like to get it put in safety. I think this is a treasure map. I thought Dr Livesey might like to see it,' I said.

'Perfectly right,' he interrupted. 'I might as well ride there.'

'Dogger,' said Mr Dance, 'take this lad.'

I mounted holding on to Dogger's belt. We struck out making for Dr Livesey's house. Blind Pew was dead in the ditch and the Captain still dead on the floor.

Groucho: Two for the price of one! Wait until their relatives get the news. Now read on. By the way, does anybody know whose dog that is?

The Captain's Papers

6

We drew up before Dr Livesey's door. I jumped down and knocked. The door was opened by a maid.

'Is Dr Livesey in?' I asked.

'No, he's gone to the Hall to dine.'

I did not remount but ran to the lodge gates. We were led down a passage to a great library, where the squire and Dr Livesey sat beside a bright fire. The horses ruined the carpet.

I had never seen the Squire Trelawney before. He had a very worn face. He must have travelled mostly on his face.

'Dance, you are a bold fellow for riding down that black, atrocious miscreant,' said the squire. 'As a magistrate I regard it as an act of violence for which you could be tried and hung.'

'And so, Jim,' said the doctor, 'you have the thing that they were after, have you?'

'Yes sir,' said I, and gave him the oilskin packet.

The doctor took it, his fingers itching to open it.

'Squire,' said he, 'Hawkins will sleep at my house. I suppose he can sup here.'

A big pigeon pie was brought in and put on a sidetable. It flew away.

'You have heard of this Flint I suppose?' asked Dr Livesey.

'Heard of him!' cried the squire. 'He was the blood-thirstiest buccaneer that sailed. He could never drink enough of it.'

'Now Jim,' said the doctor, 'we'll open the packet.'

The doctor cut the stitches with his medical scissors. It contained a book and a sealed paper.

'First of all we'll try the book,' said the doctor.

We tried it and there was nothing in it.

Finally the treasure map. The doctor opened the seals, out fell the same shit caked, Jaffa Caked map I had seen in the 'Admiral Benbow'. Further on it was written: 'Bulk of treasure here . . . The bar silver is in the north cache.

'The gold is easy found in the sand hill, N. point of north inlet cape, bearing E.'

'Treasure!' said Dr Livesey, and fainted.

'Tomorrow I start for Bristol,' the squire announced. 'In two weeks we'll have the best of ships, and the choicest crew in England. Hawkins shall come as cabin-boy.'

'Trelawney,' said the doctor, 'I'll go with you. There's only one man I'm afraid of.'

'And who's that?' cried the squire. 'Name the dog.'

Groucho: Never mind that, whose dog is he?

'You,' replied the doctor; 'for you cannot hold your tongue.'

'Yes I can,' said Trelawney, grasping hold of his tongue between his finger and thumb.

Bow wow! Bow wow!

Groucho: There it goes again! Whose dog is it?

PART TWO

The Sea Cook

I Go To Bristol

7

No longer than the squire imagined ere we were ready for the sea. The doctor had to go to London to his practice. He had to practise until he got it right. We brooded by the hour over the treasure map. When we could brood no longer we put a hen over it.

So the weeks passed away as did my Auntie Florence. The following letter arrived.

'Old Anchor Inn, Bristol, March 1, 17–'
'Dear Livesey. –
'The ship is bought and fitted. Her name is the HISPANIOLA.
'By chance I was standing on the dock, when by chance I fell in talk with a fellow. I found he was an old sailor, he smelt of rum bum and baccy and kept a public house. Long John Silver was his name. He had lost his leg and never found it.
'Through him we discovered a crew. In a few days we had a company of the toughest old salts. Those we didn't like we threw over the side.
JOHN TRELAWNEY
'P.S. Give my regards to Jim's mother. Is his father still dead?'

The next morning I arrived at the 'Admiral Benbow'. I found my mother in good spirits, my father lay no longer on his deathbed nor was the Captain lying on the floor. They had buried them both before they went off. Night passed and the next morning I said goodbye to my mother.

The mail picked us up about dusk and at dawn put us down on the dock side at Bristol.

Mr Trelawney had taken up his residence on the docks.

```
Jim:        Squire, are you a farmer?
Trelawney:  That I am, Jim.
Jim:        What do you have on the farm?
Trelawney:  Oh everything – cows, sheep.
Jim:        Do you send them for slaughter?
Trelawney:  Yes, you have to before you can
            eat 'em.
Jim:        Do you have any pets?
Trelawney:  Yes, I've a three-legged dog. His
            name is Rover but when he barks he
            falls over.
```

That night we were all aboard. We pulled up the anchor and put out to sea for sea trials. The trials involved a murderer, two arsonists and a sheep dog.

Squire Trelawney was walking the deck in a capital imitation of a sailor's walk, one step forward and three back. Some of his own servants had joined the crew, all under the command of our good ship's captain, Captain Smollett.

'So here we are,' said the squire, and so we were here.

'Soon,' I cried, 'It will be the treasure. In fact, quite soon.' It was good to know that quite soon we would find the treasure.

Groucho: It's taking a long time for them to get to me.

Q: Yes, you're playing the waiting game.

Groucho: Oh? I wondered what I was doing. What are *you* doing?

Q: I'm waiting in the wings.

Groucho: If I had wings I'd fly away over you and let you have it.

Q: You mean you'd shit on me?

Groucho: Oh you're lightning quick, you must have a high IQ.

Q: What's a IQ?

Groucho: Obviously I was mistaken.

Q: You are a difficult man with whom to get on. Apparently you don't get on with women either.

Groucho: With them I try to get off. Did you know there were no dry cleaners in Peru?

At The Sign Of
The 'Spy-Glass'

8

Out of a side room in The 'Spy-Glass' inn came the proprietor, Long John Silver. His left leg was cut off at the hip, and under the left shoulder he carried a crutch. On his right shoulder he had a parrot that blasphemed. 'Fuck all of you,' it screamed.

'Mr Silver,' I said, holding my hand out. 'My hand,' I said.

'So it is,' said Silver.

Groucho: Yes, he's got another one just like that.

'You must be Jim Hawkins,' said Silver.

'Yes, I am Jim Hawkins.'

'Now, Jim, have you ever clapped eyes on Black Dog?'

'Yes, sir.'

Just then one of the customers at the far side rose suddenly and made for the door.

'Oh,' I cried, 'stop him! It's Black Dog!'

'I don't care two coppers who he is,' cried Silver, 'but he hasn't paid his score. Harry, run and catch him.'

'Get the bastard!' shrieked the parrot.

One of the others leaped up, and started in pursuit.

'If he were Admiral Hawke he shall pay his score,' cried Silver. 'Who did you say he was?' he asked. 'Black what?'

'Black Dog, wot Churchill had,' I said. 'Has Mr Trelawney not told you of the buccaneers? He was one of them.'

'Wot, Churchill?'

'No, Black Dog.'

Standing by was Seaman Morgan. 'Now, Morgan,' said Long John, very sternly, 'I seen you talkin' with the rogue but you never clapped your eyes on that Black – Black Dog before, did you?'

'Not I, sir,' said Morgan, with a salute, poking his eye out.

'You didn't know his name, did you?'

'No, sir.'

'If you had been mixed up with the likes of him, you would never put another foot in my house. What was he saying to you?'

'Well we were a-talkin' about a recipe for curried cat,' answered Morgan.

'And now,' said Silver, 'let's see – Black Dog? Yes, I've seen the swab. I've seen him come here with a blind beggar with a face like a dog's bum with a hat on.'

'That he did,' said I. 'His name was Pew.'

'Pew!' he said. 'That was his name for certain.'

Then of a sudden he stopped and his jaw dropped. It hit the floor with a clack. He began to laugh and that so heartily, though I did not see the joke, because it wasn't funny.

The squire and Dr Livesey sat together and finished off a side of beef on the bone – and were seriously ill.

SPIKE MILLIGAN

'Well, squire,' said Dr Livesey, 'I don't put much faith in your discoveries, as a general thing; but I will say this, John Silver suits me. He will make a fine ship's cook, and he has no regard for buccaneers.'

Groucho: The fool!

Powder And Arms

9

'Now Jim,' said the doctor, 'you can go for a good sleep for the night in your hammock.' We were well out to sea, at least six feet from the quayside. The mate, Mr Arrow, was a brown old sailor with earrings in his ears and a terrible squint; he kept walking into the mast. I soon observed that things were not good between Mr Trelawney and the captain.

'Captain Smollett, sir, axing to speak with you,' said Mr Arrow.

'Alright axe! Show him in!

'Well, Captain Smollett, I hope all is shipshape?'

'Well,' said the captain, 'I had better speak plain.'

'Yes. I understand plain fluently.'

'I don't like this cruise; I don't like the men; and I don't like my officers. That's short and sweet.'

Groucho: So you don't like officers that are short and sweet?

'Then why don't you get off?' said Livesey.

'I would get off but I'd only drown. You see, I can't swim.'

'Well,' said Trelawney, 'I can't play the violin, but I don't tell everybody about it. Perhaps sir, you may not like your employer either?'

But here Dr Livesey cut in.

'Stay for a bit,' said he, 'stay for a bit.'

Groucho: I'll stay for a bit. Where is she?

'You don't, you say, like this cruise?' said Trelawney.

'Alright then, I don't say I say it,' said the captain. 'So far I find that every man before the mast knows more than I do. I don't call that fair!'

'No,' said Dr Livesey, 'I don't.'

'I have learned that we are going after treasure. Treasure is very ticklish,' said the captain.

'Then why aren't you laughing?' said Trelawney.

'It is a way of speaking,' said the captain.

'Yes, that is a way of speaking,' said Trelawney.

'I don't like treasure voyages on any account.'

'That is all clear,' replied Dr Livesey. 'Now, next you say you don't like the crew?'

'Yes, next I was going to say I don't like the crew,' said the captain. 'How did you know?'

'What about Mr Arrow?' said Trelawney.

'He's a good seaman when he's not walking into the mast.'

'Any more?' he asked.

'One more,' said the captain. 'There's been too much blabbing already.'

'Far too much,' agreed the doctor. 'It's everywhere. There's blabbing all over the deck.'

'The hands know about the treasure, so does that bloody parrot,' said the captain and he continued, 'I don't know who has this map; but I make it a point, it shall be kept secret even from me and Mr Arrow. Otherwise I would ask you to let me resign.'

'And where would you go?'

'Overboard even though I can't swim,' said the captain.

'Well,' said Trelawney, 'I can't play the violin, but I don't tell everybody about it.'

As a magistrate, he knew there was no legal limit on the number of times you could use the same joke in one book.

'I wish,' said the captain 'to make a garrison of the stern part of the ship, manned with my friend's people and provided with all the arms and powder on board.'

'In other words you fear a mutiny,' said the doctor.

Groucho:	Doesn't anybody get on with anybody on this ship?
Jim:	The voyage is fraught with danger.
Groucho:	It's worse, they've all got the clap.
Jim:	Even Mr Arrow?
Groucho:	Him especially. He didn't get that squint from walking into the mast, you know.
Jim:	Unknown to the crew the captain has piles.
Groucho:	I thought he said he had them taken away.
Jim:	Where to?
Groucho:	Somerset I think.
Jim:	Yes, that's a good place for piles.
Groucho:	How long were you in the King's Navy, Captain?

Captain: About six feet two inches.
Groucho: That's tall for a sailor.
Captain: Yes, it's also tall for a dwarf.

We were all hard at work, changing the powder and the berths, when the last man or two, and Long John along with them, came on board in a shore-boat.

The cook came up the side like a monkey, it was a brilliant disguise.

'My orders!' said the captain shortly. 'You may go below, my man. Hands will want supper.'

'Ay, ay, sir,' answered the cook; touching his forelock, he disappeared at once in the direction of his galley.

Groucho: What's this with the one-legged
 guy?
Jim: He wasn't always one-legged.
Groucho: I was going to say, shouldn't he
 have another?
Jim: Yes.
Groucho: What happened to it? Did he sell it?
Jim: It was blown off by a cannon ball.
Groucho: Did he get compensation? He could
 have made a lot of money.
Jim: It was in a war.
Groucho: Then he should sue the opposition.
Jim: It was a war against the French.
Groucho: Then he could get it in francs – all
 he needs is a good solicitor.

'You, ship's boy,' Captain Smollett cried. 'Off with you to the cook and get some work.'

I went below and Silver was bending over a saucepan of brown bubbling stuff.

Jim: Is that an Irish stew, John?

Silver: That's the current opinion, lad.

Jim: Have you had turkey for Christmas?

Silver: No I had my brother and sister for dinner.

Jim: Did they taste nice?

Silver: Delicious.

Jim: You are a strange man, John.

Silver: I used to be a strange woman till I had the operation.

Jim: Are you English?

Silver: No, Mum and Dad were Irish tinkers.

Jim: What do tinkers do?

Silver: They mend people's broken kettles. If they weren't broken, they'd break them for them first.

Jim: Didn't the owners complain?

Silver: No, it was too late. The country is full of broken kettles, Jim.

Jim: The Irish are supposed to be hot-headed.

Groucho: Oh, yes. I felt an Irishman's head once and it was very hot.

Jim: Groucho, where did you come from?

Groucho: A long line of Jews . . . that'll be another $380, please.

Jim: You make a good living.

Groucho: You call this living? Dogs have a better life than us.

Jim: A dog's life?

Groucho: Yes.

Bow wow! Bow wow!

Groucho: Whose dog *is* that?

Bow wow! Bow wow!

Groucho: You see? There it goes again. Wait a minute, it might be worse than I think. It could be *two* dogs; that or it's one dog barking twice, or two dogs barking once.

Jim: How can a man think like that?

Groucho: By living with gorillas.

Jim: You've lived with gorillas?

Groucho: How do you think I can think like that?

The Voyage

10

All that night we were in a great bustle getting stowed into place.

Groucho: Look boy, I don't want to be stowed into place – it's undignified.

'Now, Barbecue, tip us a stave,' cried one voice. ['Stave' = Middle Ages English for joke.]

'Ay, ay, mates,' said Long John, who was standing by; with his crutch under his arm, he looked deformed. 'What do you call a two foot tall Irishman? A knee Mick! Ha! Ha! Ha! Ha!'

That night as I dreamed in my hammock one end collapsed and I was knocked unconscious. I saw stars and a nursing sister from Catford.

Mr Arrow turned out far worse than the captain had hoped. He began to appear on deck with hazy eyes, red cheeks, stuttering tongue, sick down his shirt and marks of drunkenness. Sometimes for a day or two he would appear sober. We could never make out where he got the drink. One dark night, with a head sea, he disappeared overboard and was seen no more.

'Overboard!' said the captain. 'Well, gentlemen, that saves the trouble of putting him in irons.'

Actually Arrow swam ashore, won the National Lottery and married the Spice Girls, one at a time.

But there we were, without a mate; and we had to advance one of the men. The boatswain, Job Anderson, was the likeliest man. He had followed the sea all his life. Mr Trelawney had also followed the sea, but only until he caught up with it. And the coxswain, Israel Hands, was a careful, wily, old, experienced rum bum and baccy seaman.

Jim:	Israel – how did you get that name?
Israel:	I'm Jewish.
Jim:	You aren't allowed pork, are you?
Israel:	No. You know what a Jewish dilemma is Jim?
Jim:	No.
Israel:	Pork chops at half-price, ha ha.
Jim:	Were you circumcised?
Israel:	They *had* to, it was all hanging down. When the Rabbi weighed it, it was ten-and-a-half pounds!
Jim:	Captain Smollett says your wife was in prison.
Israel:	She was on the game.
Jim:	Game? What game?
Israel:	Well, let's just say it wasn't tennis, Jim.

So we just said 'It wasn't tennis, Jim.'

Jim:	Why, Hands, do you get so drunk?
Israel:	To forget.

Jim: Forget? Forget what?
Israel: Buckingham Palace.
Jim: Why? Why Buckingham Palace?
Israel: I dunno. I forgot.

Israel Hands, was a great confidant of Long John Silver, so the mention of his name leads me on to speak of our ship's cook, Barbecue, as the men called him.

Jim: Silver, how old are you?
Silver: See that oak tree?
Jim: That's three hundred years old. You're not three hundred years old.
Groucho: Not yet, Jim.
Jim: What's an oak tree doing in the middle of the Atlantic?
Groucho: Looks like the breast stroke to me.
Jim: Did you serve aboard a ship?
Silver: *HMS Warspite* – she was a good ship.
Groucho: With a *slight* tendency to sink.
Jim: Did you sail the seven seas?
Groucho: Oh more than seven – eight, nine, ten seas and seventeen oceans and twenty-eight rivers. Then he ran out of water.
Jim: Did you ever sink an enemy ship?
Silver: Yes, the *HMS Albion*.
Jim: That's a British ship!
Silver: I wondered why they shot the captain.
Jim: Did you meet any pirates?
Silver: Yes I met one in Clapham High Street.
Groucho: You must have been in great danger in Clapham High Street.

Jim: Tell me, Silver, how many brothers and sisters do you have?

Silver: At the last count eleven sisters and seventeen brothers.

Groucho: What other hobbies has your father got?

Aboard ship he carried his crutch by a lanyard round his neck, to have both hands as free as possible to strangle people. It was something to see him wedge the foot of the crutch against a bulk-head, and propped against it, yielding to every movement of the ship, get on with his cooking like someone safe ashore.

'He's no common man,' said the coxswain to me. 'He's brave – a lion's nothing alongside Long John. Once he was confronted by a lion and he knocked it to the ground. He was fined thirty shillings by the RSPCA for cruelty to animals, but he loves his parrot.'

'Cap'n Flint I calls my parrot, after the famous buccaneer.'

And the parrot would say, with great rapidity, 'Pieces of eight! pieces of eight! pieces of eight,' till you wondered that it was not out of breath, or till John threw his handkerchief over the cage. 'Take that bloody cloth off my cage!' screamed the parrot.

'Arrh, she's lovely she is,' the cook would say, and give her some sugar, and then the bird would peck at the bars and swear straight on. 'Fuck you and the crew,' cried the parrot.

'There,' said Silver, 'Here's this poor old innocent bird o' mine swearing blue fire.'

'Fuck all of you,' cried the parrot.

In the meantime, the squire and Captain Smollett were still on distant terms with each other – about a mile; the squire despised the captain. The captain, for his part, never spoke. As for the ship, he had taken a downright fancy to her. 'I have taken a downright fancy to her,' said the captain.

At this the squire would turn away and march up and down the deck, chin in air.

'A trifle more of that man,' he would say, 'and I will explode.' He had a trifle more of that man and he exploded.

What I Heard In The Apple Barrel

11

A barrel of apples had been put on deck for anybody to help himself. After sundown it occurred to me that I should like an apple. Alas, there was only one left so I dived in. I was sitting in the bottom of the barrel eating the apple when a man began to speak. It was Silver's voice, he was encouraging a mutiny. Therefore, I would not have shown myself for all the world.

To my horror Silver seemed to be in league with this mutinous crew and planned eventually to take over the *Hispaniola* and look for the treasure. He ended by saying, 'I claim Trelawney. I'll wring his calf's head off his body with these hands. Now lad, get me an apple to wet my pipe.'

My heart skipped a beat and my liver, kidneys and spleen danced a sailor's hornpipe.

'Oh don't you go sucking up apples, John. Let's go and have a rum.'

Never was I so relieved. It took half the night to clear it up.

Just then I looked up. It was night and the moon shone directly above me. Then the voice of the lookout shouted, 'Land ho!'

Council Of War

12

'And now, men,' said the captain, when all the crew was sheeted home, 'has any one of you ever seen that land ahead?'

'I have, sir,' said Silver, 'many a time. I have watered there, mostly against a tree.'

'I have a chart here,' says Captain Smollett. 'See if that's the place.'

Long John's eyes burned in his head and set fire to his hair. 'Ay, here it is: "Capt. Kidd's Anchorage."'

'Thank you, my man,' says Captain Smollett. 'I would like you later on to give us a hand.'

'Doctor,' I said, 'let me speak to you in the cabin. I have terrible news.'

'My lads,' said Captain Smollett, 'I've a word to say to you. I have to tell every man who has done his duty, alow and aloft, as I never ask to see it done better. And if you think as I do, you'll give a good sea-cheer.'

A cheer followed. It rang out so full and hearty I could hardly believe these same men were plotting for our blood.

'One more cheer for Cap'n Smollett,' cried Long John.

Groucho: Grovelling little bastard.

I went below and found the captain, the doctor and the squire. The captain was smoking with his wig on his lap which he set on fire. When he put it on it was still smoking. Quickly I told them all of the cook's intention to kill us all, take charge of the *Hispaniola* and find the treasure.

'Now, Captain,' said the squire, 'you were right, and I was wrong. I own myself an ass.'

Groucho: I wonder where he stables it?

'Captain,' said the doctor, 'Silver is a very remarkable man.'

'He'd look remarkably well hanging from a yard-arm, sir.'

Groucho: How can you look well hanging
from the yard-arm? Well hung,
perhaps . . .

'Now if it comes to blows some fine day we can count on your own home servants, Mr Trelawney?' returned the captain.

'Yes,' said the squire, 'as upon myself.'

'Three,' reckoned the captain, 'and seven counting Jim Hawkins here.'

Groucho: Three plus Jim is seven? I'm glad
you're not my accountant.

'Well, gentlemen,' said the captain, 'the best that I can say is not much.' So he said 'not much'. 'Hawkins, I put prodigious faith in you,' added the squire.

It was indeed through me that safety came. There were only seven out of the twenty-six on whom we could rely; so that the grown men on our side were six to their nineteen. They gave me a pistol which I swallowed for safety.

Groucho: Is this a first or second-class ship?
Jim: This is not a passenger ship.
Groucho: Then how do you make money?
Jim: We sell pianos.
Groucho: I know a wonderful pianist. She can't read music, so she reads the *New York Daily Herald*. Mainly the gossip column. She once played an entire concerto about Jean Harlow sleeping with Douglas Fairbanks. A man can't do much when he's sleeping.
Jim: My mother can't sleep. She's a somnambulist, she walks in her sleep.
Groucho: Where to?
Jim: My father's bed, mostly. Until he died in it.
Groucho: So where does she walk to now?
Jim: France.
Groucho: France? She'd have to swim.
Jim: No, she takes the ferry.
Groucho: Does she speak French?
Jim: She speaks a smattering.
Groucho: I wish I could speak a smattering, I'd go there.
Captain: Who is this strange man?
Jim: He says he's Groucho Marx.

Captain: What are you doing on my ship?

Groucho: I'm not doing anything on your ship.
If I did I'd clean it up.

Captain: Look, will you help us fight the
mutineers by stopping them?

Groucho: So I go up to them and say 'Stop!'
Then what?

Captain: You shoot them.

Groucho: Can't we shoot them first *then* say
stop after?

Captain: That will be too late.

Groucho: Too late? It's only three o'clock.

Captain: Three o'clock? That reminds me I
must put my watch back.

Groucho: I'm not putting my watch back. I
haven't finished paying for it yet.

Captain: Have you ever fired a musket?

Groucho: No, but I fired my secretary.

PART THREE

My Shore Adventure

How I Began
My Shore
Adventure

13

The appearance of the island when I came on deck next morning was altogether changed. Although the breeze had now utterly failed, we had made a great deal of way during the night, and were now lying becalmed about half a mile to the south-east of the low eastern coast. Grey-coloured woods covered a large part of the surface. This even tint was indeed broken up by streaks of yellow sandbreak in the lower lands, and by many tall trees of the pine family, out-topping the others – some singly, some in clumps; but the general colouring was uniform and sad.

The hills ran up clear above the vegetation in spires of naked rock. All were strangely shaped, and the Spy-glass, which was by three or four hundred feet the tallest on the island, was likewise the strangest in configuration, running up sheer from almost every side, and then suddenly cut off at the top like a pedestal to put a statue on.

Groucho: Oh God! No more boring descriptive writing, Jim. You're just holding up the book. What I want to know is what's holding me up.

The *Hispaniola* was rolling under in the ocean swell.

Groucho: My God, here he goes again!

I was a good enough sailor but this standing still and being rolled about like a bottle was a thing I never learned to stand without a qualm. Suddenly I had a qualm. The sun was very hot so we didn't touch it.

'There's a strong scour with the ebb,' said Silver, and sure enough there was a strong scour with the ebb.

The plunge of our anchor sent up clouds of birds, so the crew shot them down; but in less than a minute they were up again, whereupon they were all shot down again. Before the crew could murder the entire nesting population of the island, the captain allowed them to go ashore and I volunteered for one of the boats. Anderson was in command of my boat and instead of keeping the crew in order he grumbled.

'Well fuck,' he said, 'this is not forever.'

Groucho: No, but it's getting on that way.

If the conduct of the men had been alarming below decks, it became truly threatening when they assembled to board the boats. They lay about the deck growling together in talk. The slightest order was received with black looks, sometimes red, sometimes green.

'My lads,' said the captain, 'we've had a hot day. A turn ashore'll hurt nobody – the boats are still in the water; you can take the gigs, and as many as please can go ashore. I'll fire a gun half an hour before sundown. Hawkins, you will stay on board the *Hispaniola*.'

So I was to remain behind and watched as the shore party made their preparations. At last the party was made up. Some used lipstick, powder and rouge and they looked beautiful. Six were to stay on board, the remainder were to embark with Silver. Then it was that an idea came into my head. In a jiffy I had slipped over the side, and curled up in the foresheets of the nearest boat.

Bow wow! Bow wow!

Groucho: For God's sake, whose dog *is* that?

No one took notice of me, only the bow oar saying, 'Is that you, Jim? Keep your head down.' But Silver, from the other boat, looked sharply over and called out to know if that were me and yes it were me.

The crews raced for the beach; the bow had struck among the shore-side trees and I had caught a branch and swung myself out, and plunged into the nearest thicket, while Silver and the rest were still a hundred yards behind.

'Jim, Jim!' I heard him shouting.

I ran straight before my nose, and my nose led me to where I was now, here. And that's exactly where I was, *here.*

Groucho: Here is not a bad place to be – I mean
you could be there and then where
would you be?

Jim: Here.

Groucho: Like I said, here is a good place to
be.

Jim: How did you get here?

Groucho: I. followed you and found myself
here.

Jim: What do you hope to do?

Groucho: Nothing, so it shouldn't take long.

TREASURE ISLAND

Jim: You're a very hard man to understand.

Groucho: Okay, I'll try talking slower, but that will cost me, you know.

Bow wow! Grr! Bow wow!

Groucho: Will somebody shut that dog up!

The First Blow

14

I had crossed a marshy tract full of willows, bulrushes, and odd, outlandish, swampy trees; and I had now come out upon the skirts of an open piece of undulating, sandy country, about a mile long, dotted with a few pines, and a great number of contorted trees, not unlike the oak in growth, but pale in the foliage, like willows. On the far side of the open stood one of the hills, with two quaint, craggy peaks, shining vividly in the sun.

Groucho: I keep telling you – no more descriptive stuff; we'll never finish this job.

I turned hither and thither, hather and thather, and found myself going backwards among the undergrowth. Then I came to a long thicket of these oak-like things – I heard afterwards that they were called trees. All at once there began to be a bustle among the bulrushes; a wild duck flew up with a quack.

Groucho: That's quite normal for a duck.

Soon I heard the very distant and low tones of a human voice, I now recognised the voice as Silver's, now and again interrupted by the others. By the sound they must have been talking earnestly, and almost fiercely. At last the speakers seemed to have paused but the birds themselves began to grow more quiet; they were frightened to fly any more with the trigger-happy crew around.

Crawling on all-fours, I came into a little green dell. There I saw Long John Silver and another member of the crew come face to face.

'Silver,' said the other man, 'you're brave or I'm mistook. Will you tell me you'll let yourself be led away by this kind of messy swabs? As sure as God sees me, I'd sooner lose my hand. If I turn again my dooty –'

Far out in the marsh there arose a sound like a cry of anger then a shot followed by a long drawn-out scream ... 'Arghaaraaagagggggggghhhhhhhawwwwww!'

Groucho: Obviously he took a long time to die.

'John,' said the sailor, stretching out his hand till it reached Silver.

'Hands off!' cried Silver.

Sure enough, his hands came off.

'Hands off, if you like, John Silver,' said the other. 'But in heaven's name, tell me what was that?'

'That, Tom?' returned Silver, 'I reckon that'll be Alan.'

'Alan!' Tom cried. 'John Silver, long you've been a mate of mine but if I die like a dog ...'

Groucho: Are you the one that keeps barking?

'You've killed Alan. Kill me, too, if you can. But I defies you.' So he defied him. With that, the brave fellow turned his back and set off walking to the beach. Silver whipped the crutch out of his armpit, and sent that missile hurtling through the air. Thud!! It struck poor Tom with a stunning violence right between the shoulders. He gave a sort of gasp and fell.

Tom lay motionless upon the sward; but the murderer minded him not a whit.

'I mind not a whit,' he said hopping whitlessly over to retrieve his deadly crutch.

Now Silver put his hand into his pocket, brought out a whistle, and blew upon it several blasts. Was it half time between us? Should we change ends? He had already slain two honest people; would I come next?

Groucho: I'd say yes, but it's fifty-fifty.

I ran as I never ran before, sideways. As I ran fear grew and grew upon me, until it turned into a kind of frenzy, a kind of frenzy – a frinzy! Would not the first of them wring my neck like a chicken's?

Groucho: Yes.

It was all over, I thought. Goodbye to the *Hispaniola*. There was nothing left for me but death by starvation or death at the hands of the mutineers.

Groucho: That's sensible thinking.

A fresh sound brought me to a standstill. *Bow wow! Bow wow!* It was a dog.

Groucho: Yes, but whose dog is it?

The Man Of The Island

15

A figure appeared. What it was, whether bear or man or monkey, I could in no wise tell. It seemed dark and ragged; more I knew not. But instantly the figure reappeared, and began to head me off. From trunk to trunk the creature flitted like a deer, running manlike on two legs, but unlike any man that I had ever seen. Yet a man it was. It put the shits up me. But the mere fact he was a man had somewhat reassured me. I walked briskly towards him.

As soon as I began to move in his direction, he reappeared and threw himself on his knees. His clothes were in tatters!

'Who are you?' I said.

Groucho: Whoever he is he needs a good
          tailor.

'Ben Gunn,' he answered. His voice sounded hoarse and awkward like his balls had just dropped. 'I haven't spoke with a Christian these three years.'

'Three years!' I cried, 'Why not? Were you ship-wrecked?'

'Nay mate,' said he, 'marooned. Marooned three years agone,' he continued, 'and lived on goats since then, and berries and hamburgers and chips. You mightn't happen to have a piece of cheese about you now?'

'Do you know, for once I haven't. I've got a Swiss Army jack-knife.'

[Ben Gunn seeing Groucho –]

Ben:	Who are you?
Groucho:	If only I knew.
Ben:	Are you from the moon?
Groucho:	The nearest I got to the moon was Brooklyn. Who is this, Jim?
Jim:	Ben Gunn.
Ben:	And I'm a silly bugger.
Groucho:	Someone has to be one, unfortunately it happens to be you.
Ben:	So would you be if you'd been marooned three years.
Groucho:	Oh, my nose bleeds for you.
Ben:	Look, I don't like you.
Jim:	He means well.
Groucho:	So did Hitler.

'Now you,' he cried, 'what do you call yourself?'

'I call myself Jim Hawkins,' I said.

'Jim Hawkins?' said he. 'You've got a good memory for names. I tell you something, Jim. I am rich, rich I tell you. I am rich! I am rich!'

Jim:	You don't look rich to me. You look pretty skint.
Ben:	Do I? Have pity on a poor old bugger.

Jim: All right – so you're a poor old
bugger. You say you haven't spoke to
a Christian for three years, why?

Ben: There ain't any on the island.
Sometimes cannibals landed on the
island.

Jim: Why didn't you talk to them?

Ben: They didn't speak English; apart
from that they'd chop yer balls off
and eat you. They crapped on the
beach and I trod in it. You could
smell me for bloody miles.

Jim: I still can.

Ben: That's not the shit, that's me.

Jim: So if you're rich, I'd guess you
know where the treasure is – where
is it?

His laughing brought on a terrible fit of coughing,
combined with intermittent letting off at the back. I
waited for it to stop but it didn't. He walked backwards into the woods and then he walked forwards out
of it.

'Now, Jim, you tell me true; that ain't Flint's ship?' he
asked.

'All right, it ain't Flint's ship. Flint is dead,' I said.

'How do you know?'

'They buried him. Someone else took his place.'

'Not a man – with one – leg?' he gasped.

'Silver?' I asked.

'No, wooden,' says he.

'He's the cook; now, the ringleader too.'

'Where do you come in all this?' he said.

I told him the whole story of the voyage and the predicament in which we found ourselves.

'Ay, but you see,' returned Ben Gunn, 'what I mean is, would your Captain be likely to come down to the toon of, say, one hundred thousand pounds in treasure?'

'I'm sure he would,' said I. 'As it was, all hands were to share.'

'And a passage home?' said Ben.

'Why yes,' I cried.

'Let me tell you,' he said, 'I was here when Flint buried the treasure. He killed six of his crew. I came back on another ship and we sighted the islands. "Boys," said I, "here's Flint's treasure island; let's find it." Twelve days they looked for it and every day worse than the next. Finally they said, "As for you, Benjamin Gunn, here's a musket, and a spade. You can stay here, and find Flint's money for yourself."

'Well, Jim, three years have I been here, and not a bite of Christian diet from that day to this. But now, you look at me. Do I look like a man before the mast?'

'Not at the moment, right now you're a man before the tree.'

'Then,' he continued, 'you'll say this: Gunn-is-a-good-man-and-he-puts-a-precious-sight-more-confidence-in-a-gen'leman-born-than-in-these-gen'lemen-of-fortune,-having-been-one-hisself.'

'I don't understand one bloody word that you've been saying. How am I to get back on board?'

'Ah,' said he, 'well, there's my boat, that I made with my two hands. I keep her under the white rock. If the worst come to the worst, we might try that.'

91

Just then, although the sun had still an hour or two to run, all the echoes of the island awoke and bellowed to the thunder of a cannon.

'They have begun to fight!' I cried. 'Follow me, follow me!'

I began to run towards the anchorage. The marooned man in his goatskin trotted easily and lightly.

'Left, left,' says he. 'Keep to your left, Jim!'

So he kept talking as I ran. The cannon-shot was followed by a volley of small arms. Another pause, and then, not a quarter of a mile in front of me, I beheld the Union Jack flutter in the air above a stockade.

Narrative Continued By The Doctor: How The Ship Was Abandoned

16

SHIP'S LOG

May 4, 17–

Hunter, one of the Squire's men, Doctor and the Captain took jolly-boat to island. Found stockade whilst ashore. We heard a shot and death cry. Was it Jim Hawkins? Would he live to be 17 . . . or 18, 21 or 57?

Returned to ship. Held crew at gun point. Loaded jolly-boat with supplies and ammunition.

On deck Squire and Captain confronted mutineers.

'Mr Hands,' shouted the Captain, 'There's two of us with a brace of pistols each!'

'Oh Christ,' said Hands.

'If any of you move that man is dead.'

'Which man is that?' said Hands.

Each hoping that "that man" was one of the others, the mutineers rushed and hid below.

Signed: Smollett
Captain RN

It was about half-past-one – three bells in the sea phrase – that the two boats with the mutineers went ashore from the *Hispaniola*. The captain, the squire, and I were talking matters over in the cabin. Had there been a breath of wind we should have fallen on the six mutineers left. Down came Hunter with the news that Jim Hawkins had slipped into a boat and was gone ashore with the rest.

[Hunter – Doctor – Captain (on board ship)]

Doctor: Jim Hawkins – gone ashore? Did he swim?

Hunter: No. Somehow he smuggled himself on one of the boats.

Doctor: Good God! What was the boy thinking of?

Hunter: Well sir, he was actually thinking of his mother sleep-walking.

Doctor: Does she walk far?

Hunter: He said on one night she ended up at the Naval Barracks in Portsmouth.

Doctor: What in God's name was she doing?

Hunter: Looking for a sailor – when she met one, she said, 'Hello sailor.'

Doctor: That poor Jim, that poor boy, he's only sixteen.

Hunter: We all were once.

Doctor: Yes, we can only be sixteen once. God, what am I saying?

Hunter: Can't you remember? You were saying we can only be sixteen once.

Doctor: Yes, of course, now I remember.

Hunter: Look sir, I'll take a telescope and scan the island.

[Hunter, through his telescope, spotted Jim hiding in the bushes.]

Captain: I wonder what Jim's game is?

Hunter: I think it's football, sir.

There came a ringing cry of a man at the point of death.

'Good God,' said the Doctor, 'Jim Hawkins is gone!
He will never be 17 . . . or 18, 21 or 57!'

The squire was sitting down, white as a sheet, thinking
of the harm he had led us to.

Squire: I was just thinking of the harm I had
led you to.
Doctor: You shouldn't blame yourself. We'll
do that.

We had no time to lose. I told my plan to the captain, and
between us we settled on the details. We put Redruth, a
loyal man, in the gallery with a musket. Hunter and I loaded
the jolly-boat with supplies. By this time, tumbling things in
as they came, we had the jolly-boat loaded as much as we
dared. Joyce, another of those loyal to us, and I got out
through the stern-port, the man Gray made up the last of
our number and we made for shore as fast as we could row.

The little gallipot of a boat was gravely overloaded
with grown men, and three of them over six feet high.
Add to that powder, pork and provisions. Several times
we shipped water and the tails of my coat were soaking
wet before we had gone a hundred yards. The captain
made us trim the boat, and we got her to lie a little more
evenly. All the same, we were afraid to breathe.

'I cannot keep her head for the stockade, sir,' said I to
the Captain. 'The tide keeps washing her down. Could
you pull a little longer?'

'Not without swamping the boat,' said he.

'We'll never get ashore at this rate,' I said.

'The current's less a'ready, sir,' said Gray. 'You can
ease her off a bit.'

'Thank you, my man,' said I, quite as if nothing had happened, and indeed it hadn't.

Suddenly the captain spoke up again. I thought his voice was a little changed.

'The ship's gun,' said he.

'I have thought of that,' said I. 'They could never get the gun ashore, and if they did, they could never haul it through the woods.'

'Look astern, doctor,' replied the captain.

There, to our horror, were the rogues we had left on board busy getting off her jacket, as they called the stout tarpaulin cover under which the cannon was stowed. Not only that, but the round-shot and the powder for the gun had been left behind and it would be all put into the possession of the ones aboard. But the worst of it was, that with the course I now held, we turned our broadside instead of our stern to the *Hispaniola* and offered a target like a barn door.

'Who's the best shot?' asked the captain.

'Mr Trelawney,' said I.

'Mr Trelawney, will you please pick me off one of these men, sir? Hands, if possible,' said the captain. 'Now easy with that gun, sir, or you'll swamp the boat.'

The squire raised his gun and we leaned over to the other side to keep the balance. They had the gun slewed round and Hands, who was at the muzzle with the rammer, was, in consequence, the most exposed. Just as Trelawney fired, he stooped, the ball whistled over him, and it was one of the others who fell.

The cry he gave was echoed by his companions on board and by a great number of voices from the shore.

SPIKE MILLIGAN

Looking in that direction I saw other pirates trooping out and tumbling into their places in the boats.

'Here come the gigs, sir,' said I, 'most likely going round by shore to cut us off.'

'They'll have a hot run, sir,' returned the captain. 'It's not them I mind; it's the round shot. When you see the match, we'll hold water. You hold yours and I'll hold mine. If I dared,' said the captain, 'I'd stop and pick off another man.'

Where the ball passed, not one of us knew precisely; but it must have been over our heads and the wind of it may have contributed to our disaster. Our boat sank by the stern, quite gently, in three feet of water, leaving the captain and myself, facing each other, on our feet, with wet bollocks. We waded ashore, so far in safety, to the stockade. We landed all the stores.

No sooner was everything ashore than we set to provision the stockade. We all made the first journey, heavily laden, and tossed our stores over the palisade. Then, leaving Joyce to stand guard, we returned to the jolly-boat and loaded ourselves once more. We proceeded till the whole cargo was bestowed, and then Hunter and Joyce took up their position in the stockade.

The mutineers had the advantage of numbers but we had the advantage of arms and the bonus ball of 8.

Narrative Continued By The Doctor: End Of First Day's Fighting

17

SHIP'S LOG

May 6, 17–

Flew Union Jack above stockade. Attacked by mutineers, after sharp encounter mutineers fled leaving one of them dead. Alas, Seaman Tom Redruth mortally wounded.

May 7, 17–

Ship's cannon opened fire but the ball whistling over was behind us. We served breakfast. Took up positions at loop holes in stockade. Bombardment continued all day without harm. Made midday meal – ham, bread and some wine. Guard stood to all night calling the hours.

May 8, 17–

Flew Union Jack above stockade. Attacked by mutineers. After sharp encounter mutineers fled.

Signed: Smollett
Captain RN

Just then, with a roar and a whistle, a round-shot passed high above the roof of the log-house and plumped far beyond us in the wood.

'Oho!' cried the captain. 'Blaze away! You've little enough powder already, my lads.'

All through the evening they kept thundering away. Ball after ball flew or fell short, or kicked up the sand in the enclosure; but they had to fire so high that the shot fell dead and buried itself in the soft sand.

'There is one thing good about all this,' observed the captain; 'the wood in front of us is likely clear.'

The captain sat down to his log, and here is the beginning of the entry:

> *'Alexander Smollett, master; David Livesey, ship's doctor; Abraham Gray, carpenter's mate; John Trelawney, owner; John Hunter and Richard Joyce, owner's servants, landsmen – being all that is left faithful of the ship's company – with stores for ten days at short rations, came ashore this day, and flew British colours in the stockade in Treasure Island. Thomas Redruth, owner's servant, landsman, shot by the mutineers.'*

And at the same time I was wondering over poor Jim Hawkins' fate.

A hail on the land side.

'Somebody hailing us,' said Hunter, who was on guard.

'Doctor! Squire! Captain! Hullo, Hunter, is that you?' came the cries.

And I ran to the door in time to see Jim Hawkins, safe and sound, come climbing over the stockade. He told of a strange man called Gunn, who claimed he had found the treasure.

Narrative Resumed By Jim Hawkins: The Garrison In The Stockade

18

As soon as Ben Gunn saw Union Jack colours, he came to a halt; he was colour blind and didn't know he was white. He stopped me by the arm, and sat down.

'Now,' said he, 'there's your friends, sure enough.' He went on, 'Why, in a place like this, where nobody puts in but gen'lemen of fortune, Silver would fly the Jolly Roger. No; that's your friends. There's been blows, too, and I reckon your friends has had the best of it.'

Groucho: This guy still here?

Jim: Yes. He knows where the treasure is!

Groucho: I'm very pleased to meet you. You'll make a great film.

Bow wow! Bow wow!

Groucho: Who owns that bloody dog?

Ben: A film? – I might be dead by then.

Groucho: That's the right answer. You go to the top of the class and jump off.

Ben: What are you torkin' about?

Groucho: I'm talking about five words a second. Any faster and I'd blow the budget.

Ben: Are you mad?

Groucho: Only on Thursdays starting at midday.

Ben: You should be put away.

Groucho: I am put away, it just happens to be here.

Jim: Groucho, I must hurry on and join my friends.

Groucho: Why? Are they coming apart?

'Now,' said Ben, 'when I'm wanted you know where to find me, Jim, just where you found me today. And him that comes is to have a white thing in his hand: and he's to come alone. Oh! and you'll say this: "Ben Gunn," says you, "has reasons of his own."'

The *Hispaniola* still lay where she had anchored; but, sure enough, there was the Jolly Roger – flying from her peak. At length I thought I must return to the stockade. I skirted among the woods until I had regained the shore side of the island and was soon welcomed back by the faithful party.

The cold evening breeze whistled through every chink of the crude building, and up my trouser legs agitating my swonnicles. Sand in our eyes, sand in our teeth, sand up our backsides, and when we shit it was like concrete.

Gray, the new man, had his face tied up in a bandage for a cut he had got from the mutineers; and poor old Tom Redruth, still unburied, lay along the wall stiff and stark, under the Union Jack.

'Is this Ben Gunn a man?' asked Captain Smollett.

'That or he's queer,' I said.

'Three years on a desert island would turn anybody queer,' said the Squire.

'Was it cheese you said he had a fancy for – no rum bum or baccy?' the Captain enquired.

'Yes, sir, cheese,' I answered.

'Well, Jim,' says he, 'I don't have any cheese, but I've got a Swiss Army jack-knife.'

Before supper we buried old Tom and stood round him for a while bareheaded in the breeze. A good deal of firewood had been got in. Then, when we had eaten our pork, and each had a good stiff glass of brandy, the three chiefs got together to discuss our prospects.

It appeared they were at their wits' end what to do. We would be starved into surrender long before help came. But our best hope was to kill off the buccaneers. From nineteen they were already reduced to fifteen, two others were wounded, and one at least – the man shot beside the gun – severely wounded, if he were not dead. Every time we had a crack at them, we were to take care saving our own lives.

'So,' added the captain, 'if we are not all shot down first, they'll be glad to be packing in the schooner, and they can get to buccaneering again.'

I was dead tired, as you may fancy; and when I got to sleep, which was not till after a great deal of tossing, I slept like a log during which some silly bugger threw me on the fire.

'Flag of truce!' I heard someone say; and then, immediately after, with a cry of surprise. 'Silver himself!'

Silver's Embassy

19

SHIP'S LOG

May 9, 17–

Today Silver approached with Flag of Truce. With caution we allowed him into the stockade.

*Signed: Smollett
Captain RN*

Sure enough, there were two men just outside the stockade, one of them waving a dirty white cloth. 'It needs to be washed in Rinso,' cried the captain. The other, no less a person than Silver himself, was standing placidly by. Both waded knee-deep in a low, white, evil-smelling vapour. The island was plainly a damp, feverish, unhealthy spot.

'Don't go near them,' said the doctor, 'or we shall get damp, feverish and unhealthy in this spot.'

'Keep indoors, men,' said the captain. 'Ten to one this is a trick.'

'Who goes? Stand, or we fire!'

With that we shot off a musket.

'Flag of truce,' screamed Silver, as he ducked.

'And what do you want with your flag of truce?' cried the captain.

'Cap'n Silver, sir, to come on board and make terms,' he shouted.

'Cap'n Silver? Don't know him. Who's he?' cried the captain. And we could hear him adding to himself: 'Cap'n is he? My heart, and here's promotion.'

'Me, sir. These poor lads have chosen me cap'n after your desertion, sir,' – laying a particular emphasis upon the word 'desertion'. 'We're willing to submit, if we can come to terms, and no bones about it. All I ask is your word, Cap'n Smollett, to let me safe and sound out of this here stockade, and one minute to get out o' shot before a gun is fired.'

'My man,' said Captain Smollett, 'I have not the slightest desire to talk to you. You can come, that's all. If there's any treachery, it'll be on your side, and the Lord help you.'

'Why,' said Silver, 'there you all are together like a happy family, in a manner of speaking.'

'Yes, that's a manner of speaking,' said the captain. 'If you have anything to say, say it.'

'It,' said Silver.

The two men sat silently smoking for quite a while. They stood silently smoking for quite a while.

'Look, why don't we sit silently smoking for quite a while?' said the captain.

Occasionally Silver spat. Something would hit the ground that looked like a raw egg.

'Now,' said Silver. 'Give us the chart to get the treasure by.'

Captain Smollett rose from his seat. 'Is that all?' he asked.

Silver's face was a picture called *Titanic*; his eyes started in his head with wrath. He shook the fire out of his pipe.

'Give me a hand up!' he cried.

'Not I,' returned the captain.

'Who'll give me a hand up?' he roared.

'I'll give you a foot up,' said the captain, kicking him up the arse.

Growling the foulest imprecations, Silver crawled along the sand until he could hoist himself upon his crutch. Then he spat into the captain's eye, temporarily blinding it. Nobody at that time knew of a terrible earthquake in Italy, a whole village destroyed, 170 people killed, thousands injured.

The Attack

20

As soon as his spit-laden eye cleared Captain Smollett spoke.

'I have nothing further to say,' he said.

'Then let us use sign language,' said Silver.

The captain stuck up two fingers.

'What's that mean?' said Silver.

'In sign language it means "bugger off".'

'Well, before I bugger off,' said Silver, 'I want that treasure map.'

'First,' said the captain, 'give me your crutch.'

'But it's my only visible means of support,' said Silver.

Captain Smollett snatched the crutch from under his arm and shouted, 'Timber!'

Silver fell slowly sideways and crashed to the ground.

'I'll get you for this,' roared Silver.

'Oh?' said Smollett. 'What will you get me? How about a nice vintage red wine?'

'I'll give you vintage red wine,' snarled Silver.

'Look, Silver, I'll give you your crutch back if you get me a bottle of vintage French wine.'

With his crutch back Silver set off to find a bottle of vintage French wine. He returned to the stockade and reported to the captain.

'Captain, I've searched the island and do you think I could find a bottle of vintage French wine?'

The captain put one hand to his forehead and the other over his heart, and ran out of hands.

'For God's sake tell me if you found a bottle of vintage French wine.'

Smollett staggered back, forwards and sideways and snatched Silver's crutch. 'Timber!' he yelled.

Silver fell slowly sideways and crashed to the ground. 'I'll get you a vintage bottle of red wine for this.'

'I don't believe you any more,' said Smollett. 'I'll give your crutch back if you'll come back one by one, clapped in irons, to be taken back to England to face trial and then hung.'

Silver agreed but had no intention of coming back one by one, to be taken back to England, face trial, and then hung.

Bow wow! Bow wow! Woof woof!

'That must be somebody's dog,' said Silver.

Groucho: That's what I keep saying.

'Ah, you never were a good judge of men,' said Trelawney.

Groucho: What about women?

'Silver and his men could attack us at any time,' said the captain.

'What time is that?' said Hawkins.

Groucho: Midnight would be good for them.

'Hear that? Before the hour's out we shall be boarded. We're outnumbered, I needn't tell you that, but we fight in shelter; and I've no manner of doubt that we can drub them, if we choose.'

'Hawkins hasn't had his breakfast. Hawkins, help yourself, and back to your post to eat it,' continued Captain Smollett.

So I went back and ate my post.

'Doctor, you take the door but don't expose yourself in case there are ladies present. Hunter, take the loophole on the east side; Joyce you stand by the west side; Trelawney, you're the best shot, you guard Windsor Castle.

'Men,' said the captain.

'He means us,' said Hunter.

'Men, we are outnumbered ten to one.'

'Ten to one?' said Trelawney. 'I'll take those odds.'

'Toss out the fire,' said the captain, 'we don't want to be hindered by smoke.'

The iron fire basket was carried out bodily by Trelawney setting himself on fire. We put it out pouring bottles of vintage French red wine over him.

'Stop pouring!' shouted Trelawney, 'I can't swim.'

'Look,' said Captain Smollett, 'I can't play the violin, but I don't tell everybody.'

An hour passed away but fortunately none of us. Some seconds passed, till suddenly Joyce whipped up his musket and fired. The report had scarcely died away when there was a scattering volley, shot behind shot, like a string of geese, from every side of the enclosure. Several bullets struck the log house.

'Did you hit your man?' asked the captain.

'No.'

TREASURE ISLAND

'Load his gun, Hawkins. How many should you say there were on your side, doctor?'

'I know precisely,' said Dr Livesey. 'Three shots were fired on this side. I saw the three flashes – two close together – one farther to the west.'

'Three!' repeated the captain. 'And how many on yours, Mr Trelawney?'

Before he could answer, suddenly, with a loud huzza, a little crowd of pirates leaped from the woods on the north side, and ran straight to the stockade. At the same moment, the fire was once more opened from the woods, and a rifle-ball sang through the doorway and knocked the doctor's musket into bits. Carefully he put it together with UHU.

The boarders swarmed over the fence like monkeys. Squire and Gray fired again and yet again; three men fell, one forwards into the enclosure, two back on the outside. But of these, one was evidently more frightened than hurt, for he was on his feet again in a crack, and instantly disappeared among the trees. The doctor continued to mend his musket.

Two had bitten the dust, one had fled, four had made good their footing inside our defences; while from the shelter of the woods seven or eight men, each evidently supplied with several muskets, kept up a hot, though useless, fire on the log-house.

The four who had boarded made straight before them for the building, shouting as they ran, and the men among the trees shouted back to encourage them. In a moment, the four pirates were upon us.

The head of Job Anderson, the boatswain, appeared at the middle loophole. God knows how he managed it!

115

'At 'em, all hands – all hands!' roared the captain in a voice like thunder.

At the same moment, another pirate grasped Hunter's musket by the muzzle. 'Ahhhh!' he screamed, 'that's bloody hot.' Meanwhile a third, running unharmed all round the house, appeared suddenly in the doorway, and fell with his cutlass on the doctor. The doctor had nearly mended his musket.

'Out lads, out, and fight 'em in the open! Cutlasses!' cried the captain.

'Round the house, lads! round the house!' cried the captain; so we started to run round the house. I perceived a change in his voice, his balls must have dropped.

Next moment I was face-to-face with Anderson. He roared aloud, and his cutlass went up above his head; flashing down he cut his toe off. I had not time to be afraid, but, as the blow still hung impending, leaped in a trice upon one side, and missing my foot in the soft sand, rolled headlong down the slope.

And yet, in this breath of time, the fight was over, and the victory was ours, just as the doctor had mended his musket.

Gray, following close behind me, had cut down the big boatswain ere he had time to recover from his lost blow. Another had been shot at a loophole in the very act of firing into the house, and now lay in agony, the pistol still smoking in his hand. A third, as I had seen, the doctor disposed of at a blow. Of the four who had scaled the palisade, one only remained unaccounted for, and he, having left his cutlass on the field, was now clambering out again with the fear of death upon him.

'Fire – fire from the house!' cried the doctor. 'And you, lads, back into cover.'

In three seconds nothing remained of the attacking party but the five who had fallen, four on the inside, and one on the outside, of the palisade. The doctor and Gray and I ran full speed for shelter, went past it and had to come back again.

We saw at a glance the price we had paid for victory. It had cost us twenty-two pounds eight shillings. Hunter lay beside his loophole, stunned; Joyce by his shot through the head, never to move again; while right in the centre, the squire was supporting the captain, one as pale as the other.

'The captain's wounded,' said Mr Trelawney.

'Have they run?' asked Captain Smollett.

'All that could, you may be bound,' returned the doctor; 'but there's five of them will never run again.'

Groucho: Can I come out now?
Jim: You cowardly swine.
Groucho: Yes, that's what they all are saying. Listen!

Bow wow! Bow wow!

Groucho: See? He's still at it!

PART FOUR

My Sea Adventure

How I Began
My Sea
Adventure

21

There was no return of the mutineers. 'They have had their rations for today,' said Smollett. Out of the eight men who had fallen in the action, only three still breathed. Of these, two were as good as dead (as *good* as?); the third died under the doctor's knife, he stuck it in his heart. Hunter never recovered consciousness. He lingered all day and died, so I ate his dinner.

My own accidental cut across the knuckles was a fleabite. Dr Livesey patched it up with plaster, it set hard and I never used them again.

As for the captain, he was wounded but not badly. The wound had only displaced some muscles in his calf. He was sure to recover but he must not move his leg, swim, play rugby, hockey, or ride a bike. After dinner the squire and the doctor sat by the captain's side in consultation. Suddenly the doctor put a cake on his head, then a hot dinner over it, then his hat on and two pistols in his sock, put the map in his pocket and left the stockade. The swine! Supposing one of us gets ill?

Gray took his pipe out of his mouth. 'Where in the name of Davy Jones is he going?'

'I think in the name of Davy Jones he's going to find Ben Gunn.'

I laid hold of a brace of pistols, and as I already had a powder-horn and bullets, I felt myself well supplied with arms. I stopped; an idea came into my head. I was to go down the sandy spit, find the white rock and ascertain where Ben Gunn had hidden his boat.

The scheme I had in my head was to board the *Hispaniola*, cut her loose and guide her to the shore beyond sight of the mutineers. Then Captain Smollett and his crew could board it and sail for England. Through the bushes I observed Silver and his cut-throat gang. Suddenly his parrot began to scream, 'Old Flint the bastard is dead.' Then he whistled 'God Save the King' during which the mutineers respectfully stood to attention but I don't think they meant it.

The white rock was visible a mile away. If it had been invisible I would never have found it. Crawling on hands and knees I finally reached it. If I had stood up and walked I would have got there quicker.

By the rock was Ben Gunn's boat, well, not a boat but a coracle. It was made from goats' skin. I carried it to the water's edge, floated it, jumped in and went straight through the bottom. I quickly patched it using a Singer Sewing Machine which luckily I had found on the beach. The coracle was a perfect craft for someone of my height and weight, inside leg and shoe size.

Down I sat to wait for darkness, and made a hearty meal of biscuit.

The Ebb-Tide Runs

22

I am very sure I never should have made the ship at all but for the tide. The tide was still sweeping me down; and there lay the *Hispaniola* right in the fairway, hardly to be missed.

Soon I was alongside her hawser, and had laid hold. The hawser was as taut as a starling's bum. One cut with my sea-gulley, and the *Hispaniola* would go humming down the tide in the right direction for me. It occurred to me that a taut hawser, when cut, would suddenly become as dangerous as a kicking horse, a blow to the jaw, a club on the head, being run over by a fire-engine, stamped on by an elephant and, oh, numerous other things too terrible to be listed.

Just then a strong wind blew down at sea level. I felt the hawser slacken. I opened my gulley and cut strand after strand, after strand, after strand. Finally the vessel only swung by two.

All this time I heard the sound of loud voices from the aft cabin. One was Israel Hands and one wasn't. It was O'Brien. Both were pissed out of their heads. Even as I was listening one, with a drunken cry, opened the stern window and threw up all over me.

At last the hawser fell slack again and with my teeth and gulley I cut the last fibres. At the same time the schooner began to turn upon her heel, spinning slowly, end for end, across the current. Soon the ship was nose on for the shore in the direction of the stockade. I came across a rope hanging overboard; grasping it, I hauled myself up to the aft window. There I saw Hands and O'Brien locked together in a deadly wrestle, each one at the other's throat, sometimes at each other's nose, sometimes at each other's chin – it was terrible. A sudden lurch and I fell back into the coracle.

I opened my eyes at once. All round me were little ripples, coming over with a sharp, bristling sound. The *Hispaniola*, a few yards in whose wake I was still being whirled along, seemed to stagger in her course, and I saw her spars toss a little. As I looked longer, I made sure she also was steering to the shore.

At that time I did not know there had been terrible fires in Java burning down homes; 21 died.

The Cruise Of The Coracle

23

I was now gaining rapidly on the schooner; I could see the brass glisten on the tiller as it banged about; and still no soul appeared upon her decks. I could not choose but suppose she was deserted. If not, the men were lying drunk below, where I might batten them down.

Then of a sudden the ship came swooping down. The bowsprit was over my head. It was also over my body. With one hand I caught the jib-boom, while my foot was lodged between the stay and the brace; and as I clung there a dull blow told me the ship had struck the coracle; that's what the dull blow told me. Suddenly I knew then I was left without retreat on the *Hispaniola*.

I Strike The Jolly Roger

24

The main-boom swung inboard, catching me on the back of my head. I saw stars and a hot dog vendor from Lewisham. There were two watchmen. O'Brien lay dead on his back, as stiff as a handspike, with the arms stretched out like those of a crucifix, and his teeth showing through his open lips; Israel Hands was propped against the bollards.

While I was thus looking and wondering, in a calm moment, Israel Hands turned partly round and, with a low moan, writhed himself back to the position in which I had seen him first. The moan, which told of pain and deadly weakness, and the way in which his jaw hung open, went right to my heart. But when I remembered the talk I had overheard from the apple barrel, all pity left me.

Jim: Hands! You've had it!
Hands: No I haven't, I been at sea six weeks.
Jim: Doing what?
Hands: Killing O'Brien, ha, ha!
Jim: Why did you kill him?
Groucho: He wouldn't stop telling him Irish jokes.

Hands: I'd heard them all before.

Jim: Groucho! Where did you come from?

Groucho: I keep asking myself that.

Hands: Don't let Jim kill me.

Groucho: Do you intend to kill him?

Jim: No.

Groucho: How's that for service?

Hands: God bless you, sir.

Groucho: I've never been called sir before, it's usually been 'Hey you, shit face!'

'Are you alive, Hands?' I said. He and his blood-covered body answered 'Yes,' and collapsed with effort.

I asked him if he would like to dance the tango. Sportingly he said 'No.'

Groucho: Oh, don't be a spoil sport.

He drummed up enough strength to say 'Brandy'. Shopping around I found a bottle of it in Harrod's Wine Department. He must have drunk a gill before he took the bottle from his mouth – it was trickling out the back.

'Aye,' said he, 'by thunder, but I wanted some o' that! Where do 'ee come from?'

Groucho: I keep asking myself that.

Jim: He's a murderer, Groucho.

Groucho: A solicitor needs him.

Jim: You mean he needs a solicitor.

Groucho: No, the solicitor needs him, he's got to make a living.

'I've come to take possession of the ship,' I said. Next I ran down the Jolly Roger, and hoisted the Union Jack. 'God save the King,' I said.

'Fuck the King,' said Hands.

'Look,' he said, so I looked. 'You'll be wanting to go ashore,' he said.

'Yes,' I said. 'But I'm not going back to Captain Flint's anchorage. I mean to take her to North Inlet and beach her.'

He nodded. 'Aye, get me more brandy and I'll teach you how to steer the ship.'

So I gave him some brandy and he taught me how to steer the ship. In three minutes I had the *Hispaniola* sailing before the wind. I lashed the tiller, went below and got a soft silk handkerchief of my mother's that she gave me when she wasn't sleep walking. I bound Hands' wounds.

'God bless 'ee,' said Hands, so God blessed me.

After he had a swig of brandy he began to pick up. First he picked up some rubbish on the deck. Then he picked up a copy of *Newsweek*. Yet his eyes followed me around the deck and then they rolled back to him. He gave me a comfortable smile, but he was filled with treachery and rum bum and baccy.

Israel Hands

25

'This 'ere is an unlucky ship, Jim. We've tried the National Lottery five times but won bugger all,' he said.

He drank some more brandy. By now he was really pissed. He staggered into the mast and lay unconscious; flies settled on his face and crapped on him. I continued to steer the ship. He came to.

'Ah, O'Brien,' he slurred, ' 'ee's dead.'

Groucho: That or he's a brilliant actor.

'Yes, he's in another world,' I said, 'and watching us.'

Groucho: God, he must have wonderful eyesight.

'Look, Captain,' said Hands. 'Could you get me some wine? The brandy is doin' me.'

For some reason he wanted me below deck. 'Wine?' I said. 'What would you like? A Chablis or a Mouton Rothschild?'

'Yes' he said.

I scuttled below. I mounted the forecastle and popped my head out of the fore companion. He had got possession of a blood-stained knife, then hid it on his person. I returned on deck with a bottle of wine. I felt sure I could trust him on one point – we both wanted the ship beached. Hands had adopted his original position, his head hung down as if he were too weak to move.

Groucho: Look out, Jim, he's acting!

Hands snatched the bottle, knocked the neck off and drained it. 'Here, cut me a chunk off this stick of tobacco.' So I cut him a chunk off his stick of tobacco. 'Now look 'ere,' said Hands.

Groucho: Yes, Jim, look here. There's a nice bit to beach the ship in.

'Starboard a little – steady – starboard – starboard – starboard a little – steady!' He issued commands which I breathlessly obeyed. All of a sudden he cried, 'Now, my hearty, luff!' And I put the helm hard over; the *Hispaniola* went hard on to the sandy beach.

Perhaps I had heard a creak or seen his shadow moving with the tail of my eye.

Groucho: Your eye's got a tail? So's my dog but it's the other end.

Suddenly the *Hispaniola* struck, staggered, ground for an instant in the sand. We almost rolled together into the scuppers, Groucho, Hands and I. Hands jumped to his feet.

Groucho: Look out, Jim, he's got a duck!

Sure enough, there was Hands half-way towards me with the dirk in his hand.

Groucho: A dirk? Don't you mean a duck?

Jim: No, Groucho, you can't be stabbed with a duck.

Groucho: Are you sure, Jim? A friend took me to a restaurant once and I got stuck with the bill!

Hands raised the duck over his head and lunged at me. I leapt sideways, drew a pistol from my pocket and, as he stabbed at me with his duck, I pulled the trigger. The hammer fell, there followed no flash – it was useless with sea water. He continued to threaten me with his duck. Quick as thought I sprang into the mizzen shrouds, rattled up hand-over-hand, and did not draw a breath till I was seated on the cross-trees.

The duck had struck not half a foot below me. Below me Hands climbed with his mouth open; I threw a musket ball in it; it went right through him. I lost no time in re-priming my pistols, and pointing them at him I said, 'One more step, Hands, and I'll blow your brains out!'

Groucho: No, he hasn't got any.

'Jim,' said Hands, 'I reckon we're fouled, you and me, and we'll have to sign articles.'

I listened to his words with a smile.

Suddenly with the speed of light, back went his right hand over his shoulder, something sang like an arrow through the air, I felt a blow then a sharp pang. I was pinned by the shoulder by the duck. Both my pistols went off and fell from my hands. They did not fall alone; with a choked cry Hands fell from the shrouds and plunged into the sea.

Groucho: He's fallen into the water.
Hands: Help! Help! I can't swim!
Groucho: Listen, I can't play the violin but
I don't shout about it. See if this
will help.

So saying, Groucho threw a cannon ball on him. He
sank without trace. He was dead, wounded, shot,
stabbed and drowned.

'*Pieces Of Eight*'

26

My first thought was to pluck forth the duck that pinned me to the mast. I threw some duck food on the deck and he immediately flew down, ate it and died. It was poisoned.

Groucho: Jim? You've poisoned the duck. Wait until the RSPCA hear of this.

I threw O'Brien over the side. The Irishman had never been taught to drown, so Groucho threw another cannon ball on him.

'I'd better be getting ashore and back to the stockade,' I said.

I looked over the side; the water looked shallow. I jumped in; the water was up to my waist. At last I was off the sea, nor had I returned empty handed. There lay the *Hispaniola* ready for our own men to board again. I became aware of a red glow against the sky.

Groucho: I, myself, have nothing against the sky. It's never done me and my family any harm.

Suddenly right in front of me a glow appeared on the trees. It was red and hot as if it was the embers of a bonfire smouldering. For the life of me I could not think what it was. It was the embers of a bonfire smouldering. Suddenly a brightness fell on me. Of course, it was the moon.

Groucho: One day man will walk on it.
Jim: I don't believe you.
Groucho: I knew I'd have trouble convincing you.

At last I came to the stockade itself. As I drew nearer, I heard a heartening sound; it was Captain Smollett and his crew snoring. Well, one or some of his crew.

Groucho: It's just as well not to blame everybody. Some may not be snoring and are innocent!

With my arms before me I walked forward steadily. I should lie down on my own place and enjoy their faces when they found me in the morning. My foot struck something – it was a sleeper's leg. And a shrill voice in the darkness, 'Pieces of eight! Fuck!' It was Silver's parrot.

I had no time to recover. The sleepers awoke. With a mighty oath a voice shouted, 'Who the fuck is that?' It was Silver.

I turned to run straight into the arms of a mutineer.

'Bring a torch, Dick,' said Silver.

And one of the men left the log-house and presently returned with a lighted brand.

Groucho: Watch out Jim, they're going to set fire to you!

PART FIVE

Captain Silver

In The Enemy's Camp

27

I realised the mutineers were in possession of the stockade and me.

Groucho: But is it insured against Fire, Floods or Earthquakes?

Six was all that was left of them. One lay on his bed, a blood-stained bandage round his head which told that he had recently been wounded, and still more recently dressed.

The parrot sat on Long John's shoulder which was covered in parrot's crap. He himself looked paler and more stern. Was it the parrot's crap?

'Now Jim,' said Silver, 'as you are here, I'll give you a piece of my mind.'

I took it and thanked him for it.

'What has happened to all my friends?'

'You can't go back to your lot,' said Silver. 'They won't 'ave you and the doctor's dead against you. "Ungrateful scamp" is what he said.'

Thank heaven my friends were still alive, but incensed at my 'desertion'.

'Lad,' said Silver, 'no one's a-pressing you.'

Sure enough, none of them were a-pressing me.

'I've a right to know where my friends are.'

'Wot's wot?' snarled one of the mutineers. 'You'd be a lucky one as knowed that.'

'Well, I am lucky,' I said, 'so I knowed that.'

'Batten down your hatches,' said Silver to the mutineer.

'Fuck you, Silver,' he said.

'And fuck you, too,' said Silver.

Groucho: What a witty tongue he has.

'Yesterday,' said Silver, 'love was such an easy game to play. Yes, yesterday Dr Livesey came down with a flag of truce. "Captain Silver," he said, "You've sold out. The ship's gone." We looked out, and there, sure enough, was the ship, gone!

' "Well," says the doctor, "let's bargain."

' "How many are you?" says I.

' "Four," says he, "and one of us wounded. As for that lad, we don't know where he is!" '

'Is that all?' I asked.

'Yes, that's all you are to hear,' said Silver.

'I have a thing or two to tell you,' I said.

'Yes, tell me a thing or two,' said Silver.

'Well, the schooner, I cut her loose, and I . . .' I said, thumping my chest, giving me a fit of coughing. 'I, what was I saying?'

'You were saying you cut her loose,' said Silver, handing me a cough sweet.

'Yes, then I killed the men you left aboard. You'll never never find the ship. Now, Mr Silver, I take it you will tell the doctor my story?'

'All right,' said Silver, 'you little bastard.'

'That little bastard,' said Morgan who knowed Black Dog!' And he sprang up, drawing his duck.

Silver sprang to his feet – in his case, his foot. 'Who are you, Morgan! Don't you cross me.'

Morgan, a religious man, crossed himself.

Groucho: Why not? He's crossed everybody else.

A hoarse murmur came from the others.

'Morgan's right,' said one, two and three. 'The lad's not one of us and neither's anyone that stands with him!'

'Well,' snarled Silver, 'I'm ready. Take a cutlass him that dares.'

Not a man stirred, not a man answered.

Groucho: You've given them the shits.

'That's your sort, is it?' Silver took his pipe from his mouth and spat at what looked like a bowl of porridge hiding on the floor. 'Well, you're a gay lot,' said Silver.

Groucho: Thanks for the warning.

They, for their part, moved to the end of the stockade.

Groucho: Not much of a part.

A low hiss emanated from them. I thought one of them had a puncture. Occasionally they would look at Silver.

'Wot are you saying?' said Silver, spitting high in the air, landing it on a mutineer's head.

'You dirty bastard,' he shouted.

'Pipe up. Let's hear wot you got to say.'

'We haven't said anything, we've only been hissing,' they said.

'Ax yer pardon?' said one.

'All right, ax,' said Silver.

'I ax yer pardon,' said one. 'Accepting you for to be captain I claim my right to step outside for a council.' So saying, they all stepped outside for a council.

The sea cook instantly removed his pipe from his mouth.

Groucho: It'd been in worse places.

'Did you see that, Jim?' said Silver.

'Yes, you removed your pipe from your mouth,' I said.

'Now look you here, Jim Hawkins,' said the sea cook.

So I looked here.

Groucho: Can you see anything there?

'You're within a plank of death,' said Silver. 'They're going to throw me off.'

Groucho: Will it be Beachy Head or the GPO Tower?

'But you stand by me, Hawkins, and I'll stand by you,' said Silver.

'You mean all is lost?' I asked.

'Aye, by gum I do,' he answered. 'Understand me, Jim, I've a head on my shoulders,' said Silver.

Groucho: It's a good place for it.

Silver drew some cognac from the cask and poured it into a bicycle, which he drank through the handle-bar, then rode it round the stockade stopping now and then to take a sip from the handle-bar.

Groucho: You shouldn't drink and drive.

Silver shook his great shaggy head, like a man who looks forward to the worst. The very worst is death.

The Black Spot Again

28

The council of mutineers lasted a long time.

Groucho: A year to be exact.

They were collected in a group; one held a light, another held a tree, and another held a cow. He also held a bible. The party moved towards us.

'Here they come,' said I, and here they came.

'Let 'em come,' said Silver. 'I've still got a shot in my locker.'

'What good is that?' I said.

'I don't rightly know,' said Silver.

Five of the mutineers approached, one holding his closed hand in front of him.

'You can't fool us,' said a mutineer.

Groucho: Why not? I've fooled everybody
          else.

'Hand it over, lubber,' said Silver, taking another sip from the handle-bar.

The mutineer passed something to Silver.

'The black spot, ha, ha,' said Silver. 'This black spot 'as been cut from the Holy Bible. What fool's cut a Holy Bible?'

'Ah there,' said Morgan. 'Wot did I say? No good'll come o' that.'

'Well, you've fixed it now,' continued Silver. 'What bloody fool cut the Holy Bible?'

'It was Dick,' said one.

'Dick was it?' said Silver. 'He's seen his slice of luck go.'

There a long man with yellow eyes spoke. 'Belay that talk, Silver. We tipped you the black spot, ha ha. See what's written on the back.'

Silver read it. ' "Book of Kings, Chapter I, verse 17. And lo Christ went unto Galilee and a great crowd gathered." '

Groucho: Anyone sad enough to have looked up
that quote and found it's wrong –
get a life!

'Below that, Silver,' said yellow eyes.

Silver read, 'Step down.'

'Come now, Silver,' said George, 'You're a funny man.'

Groucho: Yes, tell 'em a joke.

Silver rode his bicycle round the mutineers, occasionally taking a drink from the handle-bar.

'Look, just dismount from that bicycle and help us vote.'

'Listen,' said Silver, 'I'm still your captain till you outs with your grievances; till then I shall continue to ride my bike and drink from the handle-bar.'

'You let the enemy out of this 'ere stockade for nothing. Then there's this 'ere boy,' said George.

'Is that all?' said Silver.

'Enough, too,' said George, doing a back somersault, landing on his feet. 'We'll all swing for your bungling.'

'Who forced my hand to be captain? Who tipped me the black spot, ha, ha cut from the Holy Bible with Book of Kings written on the back?'

'Go on, John,' said Morgan doing a back somersault landing on his feet. 'Speak up to the others.'

'Maybe,' said Silver, refilling his bike with cognac, 'you don't count for nothing, a *real* doctor come to see you every day – you John, with your head broke – or George Merry, with ague shakes, and you, Morgan, with swollen balls and the shits, all for free.

'And as for the boy, we will be glad we got a hostage when the time comes,' said Silver.

And he cast down a paper that I immediately recognised as the treasure map. Why the doctor had given it to him was more than I could understand. The mutineers leaped upon it like a cat upon an elephant (mouse?). And by the oaths and childish laughter you would have thought not only were they fingering the very gold, but were at sea with it, in safety.

Suddenly they stopped. They were not fingering the gold, they were not at sea in safety; no, they were all still stuck in the stockade with Silver riding his bike around them.

'Oh, let's have a go, Silver,' said Morgan.

'Just this once,' said Silver.

One by one the mutineers took turns to ride and drink from the handle-bar, finally all falling into a drunken sleep.

It was long ere I closed my eyes that night. Before I did, I thought of my mother sleep walking and wondered where she was. [That night she had reached Billingsgate Fish Market.]

Silver himself slept peacefully and snored aloud. My heart was sore for him, wicked as he was, to think of his perils ahead, and – the gibbet that awaited him.

Groucho: Oh, an unhappy ending. Stay asleep, Silver; when you wake you'll be hung.

On Parole

29

I was awakened by a gentle kick to my head by Morgan. I could see the semi-sober sentinel shake himself together; he fell in bits on the floor. Remembering his duty he called out the time, 'One o'clock and all's well.' He was seven hours late.

'Stockade ahoy!' said a hearty voice.

'Here's the doctor,' said Silver from his bed. 'He must have come here in the dark. His face is covered in bruises through walking into trees.

'You, Doctor, top of the morning to you,' said Silver from his bed.

'George, shake yourself, help the doctor over the ship's side,' said Silver.

'Don't let that smelly bugger touch me, I don't want to catch it,' said the doctor.

'We've quite a surprise for you,' said Silver rising from his bed. 'We've a little stranger here, a noo lodger rent free.'

'Rent free?' said the doctor. 'You're a fool.' The doctor paused. 'Wait, you don't mean – Jim Hawkins?'

'I *do* mean Jim Hawkins,' said Silver moving towards the doctor and colliding with him.

The doctor seemed stunned by the news which had been broadcast that night by the BBC overseas programme.

'Is he safe?' said the doctor.

'Alive and well,' said Silver.

'Well, well,' said the doctor, 'Duty first. Let's overhaul these patients of yours.'

He proceeded towards the 'Sick Bay'. He went among them as though it was a visit to a quiet English family.

'Ah, you're doing well, John,' he said to the bandaged head. 'If ever a person had a close shave it was you.'

'Yes, it *was* me,' said John.

'Your head must be hard as iron,' said the doctor.

'Yes, it is,' said John.

'Well, you, George, you're a terrible colour. Your liver must be upside down.'

'It is, sir,' said George.

'Ah, Morgan, you've got swollen testicles.'

'No sir, I've got swollen balls.'

'That as well?' said the doctor. 'Well every day dip them in cold water three times a day. You've got varicocele.'

'What's that?' said Morgan.

'Swollen Balls,' said the doctor.

'Got the shits as well,' said Morgan.

'Have you any porridge?' said the doctor. 'Eat a big bowl every morning.'

'So I dips me balls in cold water three times a day, and eat porridge every morning?' said Morgan.

Groucho: You've something to look forward to.

'Dick don't feel well,' said Silver.

'I can give you some pills for that,' the doctor replied.

'No, I mean him,' said Silver, pointing to Dick. 'He don't feel well.'

'Doesn't he?' said the doctor. 'Well, step up, lad, let me see your tongue. God, this tongue is enough to frighten the French fleet. No, I'm afraid he must be put to bed. He has Swamp Fever; give him these tablets morning and night.'

The news seemed to alarm the mutineers.

'Is it contagious?' said one.

'Very,' said the doctor, putting his medicines back in his bag.

'Dick is sick,' said Morgan, ' 'cause he spoiled his Bible.'

'Nonsense,' said the doctor. 'It's not knowing honest air from poison. Camp in a bog, did he? Silver, you don't seem to have a notion of the rules of health. Before long you'll all die of swamp fever, typhus, plague, chilblains and piles. Can I now speak to the boy?'

Silver turned to Hawkins. 'Hawkins, will you give me your word of honour not to slip your cable?'

I gave readily the pledge.

'Then, Doctor,' said Silver. 'Step outside. I'll bring the boy to you.'

We advanced to where the doctor awaited. 'You'll make a note, Doctor, that I saved this boy's life.'

The doctor jotted down in a note book, 'Remember Silver saved boy's life. Pick up dry cleaning. Buy milk.'

The doctor nodded his head but it didn't fall off.

'Jim, you're not afraid?' said the doctor.

'Doctor, spare me. I blame myself for my situation. I'd been dead by now if it hadn't been for Silver. What I fear is torture.'

'Yes,' said the doctor, 'I've made a note of it.

'Jim,' said the doctor, 'I can't stand this – let's run for it.'

'No, I've given my word,' I said.

'I know, I know,' he cried. 'We can't help that. Let's run for it like antelopes.'

'I can't run for it like antelopes. I gave my word, but if they torture me I won't tell where the ship is. It lies in the North Inlet on the Southern beach.'

'The ship?' exclaimed the doctor.

Rapidly I described my adventures.

'It's you that saved our lives, Jim. Silver,' he cried as the cook drew near, 'don't be in a great hurry to find that treasure.'

'Why sir, I do my possible, which that ain't.'

The doctor didn't understand that, neither did I.

'I'll give you hope, Silver,' said the doctor. 'If you get alive out of this wolf-trap,' said the doctor, 'I'll do my best to save you.'

Silver didn't know he was in a wolf-trap, but he was grateful.

'You couldn't say more if you were my own mother.'

'Silver, I am not your mother. My advice is, keep the boy close beside you and if you need help, shout halloo. Good-bye, Jim,' he said, and he turned and walked into a tree.

Bow wow, Grrr, Woof woof!

Groucho: My God, he's getting more confident.

The Treasure Hunt
– Flint's Pointer

30

'Jim,' said Silver, 'if I saved your life, you saved mine, I'll not forget it.'

Yes, he would not forget it, he said so.

'Now, we're going on this treasure hunt. You and me must stick close, back to back.'

Groucho: You won't get very far in that position.

'We'll find the treasure and we'll save our necks.'

Groucho: Only your necks? Not much to look forward to, eh?

A mutineer called us saying breakfast was ready. It was roast turkey, shot in the bush.

Groucho: What a terrible death.

'I've just eaten three times more than I couldn't eat,' said Silver, swallowing the parson's nose.

Groucho: My man, what has the parson got to say about this?
Jim: Listen, it wasn't the parson's, it was the turkey's.

Groucho: Oh? What's a turkey doing with a parson's nose? Hasn't he got one of his own?

Jim: Please go away, Groucho, and die.

Groucho: I'll have to think about that. Now whose dog is this?

Bow wow! Bow wow!

Groucho: Believe me, you'll miss me.

A mutineer was throwing masses of food away on the fire as though there was no tomorrow.

Groucho: Yes, there is a tomorrow, just you wait and see!

'Aye mates,' said Silver, 'Lucky you 'as me to think for you with this here head. Sure enough they got the ship, but once we hit the treasure, we'll find it.'

No wonder the men were in good humour. I was terribly cast down.

Groucho: Cheer up, Jim, let me terribly cast you up.

Silver still had a foot in either camp.

Groucho: And that's no mean feat with only one foot!

'If the mutineers do attack us, there's Silver, a cripple, and only me, a boy,' I said.

Groucho: I'll give a hundred to one you'll lose.

We made a strange group of people, all but me armed to the teeth.

Groucho: Why do people want to arm their
teeth?

Silver had four pistols – one in front, one at the back,
one in his sock and one under his hat. 'Let 'em come
one come all,' he growled.

At his waist Silver had a cutlass. His parrot was still
on his shoulder, ankle deep in parrot shit, still talking.
'Avast ye lubbers, get below!!!'

Groucho: Don't get below him, he'll shit all
over you.

With a rope around my waist, I followed after Silver
who held the loose end in his teeth.

I gave the rope a sharp pull and out shot Silver's teeth.
'Dwon't byou bever bdo bthat bagain,' he mumbled.

Groucho: Give him his teeth back or he'll
never talk again.

Silver returned his dentures back, but wait! His face
had gone a funny shape.

Groucho: My God, he's put them in upside
down!

Silver reversed his teeth and his face fell back into
place.

So we all set out for the treasure, even the fellow with
the bandaged head and the one with the shits and the
swollen balls, and struggled one after another to the
beach. We jumped on the long-boat and soon we were
pulling out to sea, heading for the point near the
treasure.

Groucho: You men don't mind me travelling as a stowaway? Are these the first class planks?

We pulled easily by Silver's directions with Groucho hanging on behind. We consulted the map:

TALL TREE. SPYGLASS HILL BEING A POINTER TO N. OF NE.
SKELETON ISLAND ESE., AND BY E.
TEN FEET.

Groucho: Who's got ten feet? He could make a fortune in the circus. Does he have an agent?

'We'll only find this spot,' said Silver, 'by reading the compass.'

Groucho: I only read the *Sun* for its page three boobs.

After a long passage, we landed at our chosen place. We began to ascend the slope towards a plateau. At the first onset, heavy, heavy, miry ground, matted, marshy vegetation, snakes, lions, tigers and gorillas delayed our progress.

Groucho: Don't forget the quicksands, which I am in at the moment.

'Stay there,' said Silver. 'We'll collect you on the way back.'

Groucho: Wait! I might have disappeared by then!

We had gone half a mile when the man farthest away began to shout in terror. The reason was he was standing over a skeleton.

' 'ee's dead,' said Morgan. 'But what sort of way is that for bones to lie? T'aint natural.'

Indeed at a glance the man lay perfectly straight, his hands raised above his head like a direction pointing directly ahead.

'I've taken a notion into my old numbskull,' observed Silver.

The body pointed straight in the direction and the compass pointed ESE and by E.

'I thought so,' said Silver. 'This 'ere is a pointer. Right up there is a line for the pole star and the jolly dollars!'

'This skeleton was Allardyce, he owed me money,' said Morgan.

Groucho: Looks like you won't get it back. Does anyone know if dry cleaning takes out quicksand stains?

'He stole my duck and he was killed by Flint,' said Morgan.

'Come, come,' said Silver, 'stow this talk. Flint's dead. Let's head for the treasure.'

The mention of Flint had an effect on the mutineers. They spoke with bated breath. The terror of Flint grew on them.

Groucho: If it grew on me I'd chop it off.

The Treasure Hunt
– The Voice
Among The Trees

31

'I don't feel sharp,' said Morgan. 'Thinking of Flint gives me the shits.'

Groucho: Then don't you come near me.

All of a sudden a ghostly voice came from the middle of the trees.

Fifteen men on the dead man's chest —
Yo-ho-ho, and a bottle of rum!

'It's Flint, by –!' cried Merry.
Yes, it was Flint, by –!
The song stopped as suddenly as it began.
'Darby M'Graw,' it wailed, 'Darby M'Graw, Darby M'Graw.'
'That's Flint all right,' said Merry. 'Let's all fuck off.'
'Thems was 'is last words,' said Morgan, 'Let's fuck off.'
Dick had his bible out and read ' "And Jesus walketh on the water." '
'Bollocks,' said Morgan, ' 'ee would 'ave drowned!'
'Shipmates!' shouted Silver, 'I'm here to get that treasure. I never was feared of Flint. There's seven hundred thousand pounds not a hundred yards from

here! That weren't Flint's voice, it had an echo now. Spirits don't have an echo. By the power!' shouted Silver, 'it were Ben Gunn, the silly bugger.'

'Why, nobody minds Ben Gunn; he's a silly bugger,' said Morgan.

Suddenly the mutineers' spirits had returned. They put their tools on their shoulders and set forth again.

Groucho: Tools on their shoulders? They must be deformed.

Merry walked first with Silver's compass.

Dick alone clutched his bible, looked around him with fearful glances; Silver even joked him on his precautions.

'Who makes all the ice cream in Israel? Walls of Jericho! Ha-ha!'

But Dick was not comforted; it was plain he was falling sick. His temperature was growing higher; finally he started to smoulder, then burst into flames and fell to the ground. There was no water so they all urinated on him to put it out.

The first of the trees reached proved the wrong one; 'Fuck,' said Morgan. So was the second; again 'Fuck,' said Morgan. The third tree rose two hundred feet in the air – how it got up there we never knew. But it was not that that impressed them, it was the knowledge that seven hundred thousand pounds lay in its shadow.

Silver hobbled on his crutch; he cursed when flies in swarms settled on his nose. It was hard to keep up with the rapid pace of the treasure-hunters, who were moving at fifty miles per hour. Dick was lying on the ground a smouldering mound stinking of piss.

Bow wow! Bow wow!

Groucho: Good God, he's *still* here!

We were now at the margin of the thicket.

'Huzza, mates, all together!' shouted Morgan; and the foremost broke into a run, the foremost arrived first.

And suddenly, not ten yards further, a low cry arose. Silver doubled forward.

Before us was a great excavation, not very recent, for the sides had fallen in and grass had started to grow on the bottom.

Groucho: Grass is growing on whose bottom?

In this was the shaft of a pick broken in two, and the boards of several packing cases strewn around and an old hamburger and chips. One of these boards had been branded with a hot iron; on it was the word *Walrus* – the name of Flint's ship.

All was clear. The treasure had been found and rifled; the seven hundred thousand pounds were gone. They all said 'Fuck!'

Groucho: Look on the bright side, boys. You can get unemployment benefit.

The Fall Of A Chieftain

32

Each of these six men was as though he had been struck. With Silver the blow passed instantly.

'Jim, take that and stand by for trouble.'

So saying he passed me three pistols from under his hat. At the same time he began retreating until he had put the hollow between us and the mutineers. He looked at me as if to say, 'Here is a tight corner.'

Groucho: Right now you're five hundred to one.

The mutineers, with oaths and cries, leaped into the pit to dig with their fingers, throwing aside boards as they did. One ate the old hamburger and chips. Morgan found a piece of gold; he held it up with a stream of 'Fucking hell! What the fuck is this?'

'Two bloody guineas!' roared Merry. 'That's your seven hundred thousands is it, Silver?'

'No it isn't,' said Silver, 'it's two bloody guineas.'

'You're the man for bargains, are you?'

Groucho: Yes, he shopped modestly and only went to auctions.

'Mates, I tell you,' screamed Merry, 'I tell you now – that man there knew it all along. I look on the face of him and you'll see it wrote there.'

Sure enough, written on Silver's forehead was 'That man there knew it all along.' By this time everyone was in Merry's favour. They began to scramble out of the excavation, but on the opposite side. Well, there we stood, two on one side, five on the other.

At last Merry seemed to think a speech might help. He cleared his throat, it landed on the other side. 'Ladies and Gentlemen, unaccustomed as I am to public speaking,' he began. 'Men,' he said raising a cutlass in his hand, 'follow –'

Just then, crack! crack! crack! Three musket shots flashed out of the thicket.

Groucho: It's the Twelfth Cavalry.

Merry tumbled head first into the pit; the man with the bandaged head spun round, dead.

The remaining mutineers fled in the direction of away. Before you could wink, we were joined by the doctor, Gray and Ben Gunn, the silly bugger.

'Forward!' said the doctor, 'we must head them off before they reach their long-boat.'

We set off at a pace of fifty miles an hour. Silver followed us at the lesser speed of forty; oh, the agony that he went through till the muscles of his chest were fit to burst; in fact the muscles of his chest did burst and he came out. It took him ages to scoop himself back in again and rebutton his doublet after which a shrill little voice could be heard from inside screaming, 'Pieces of eight! Fuck you!' He was already thirty yards behind us and on the verge of collapse.

'Doctor,' he called, 'I'm on the verge of collapse; there's no hurry.'

Sure enough, we were between the mutineers and their boat so we sat down to catch our breath. Mind you, you can catch your breath standing up but we were doing it further down.

Long John joined us. 'Thank 'ee doctor; you came in the nick-o-tine. So it's you, Ben Gunn the silly bugger.'

'Yes, I'm Ben Gunn,' said the marooned 'silly bugger'.

'Ben Gunn, you silly bugger, you had the treasure all the time!'

Ben Gunn, the silly bugger, had found the treasure and carted it back to his cave. It took him two years to do it.

'Yes, I went all around the island. I took it to my cave, but I couldn't find anywhere to spend it!'

Silver laughed. 'Ha ha, don't worry, we'll find somewhere.'

We found the mutineers' boat and smashed it into teeny-weeny pieces.

'Ah,' said Silver, 'it was fortunate for me I had Jim Hawkins here. You would let old John be cut to bits, and never give it a thought, Doctor.'

'No,' said the doctor, 'even if you were cut to teeny-weeny bits.'

Groucho: Using a scalpel, I presume?

We all made for Ben Gunn, the silly bugger's cave. The squire met us. At Long John's salute, he flushed. Someone had pulled his chain.

'John Silver,' he said, 'you're a prodigious cook, villain, imposter, thief, murderer, mimic and a bank manager, sir.'

Groucho: Making seven all together.

'Thank you for me being all those,' said Silver.

After a long walk we entered the cave; before a big fire lay Captain Smollett and in the far corner a great heap of silver doubloons and quadrilaterals of solid bars of gold. At the sight of it the doctor fainted.

'It's too much for him, but it's not too much for me,' said Silver excitedly.

Little did we know that at that moment there were terrible floods in Bangladesh with 32 drowned.

'Now you, John Silver,' said the captain, 'what brings you here, man?'

'I was carried here by Ben Gunn,' returned Silver.

'God forgive you for being a scoundrel,' said the captain. So God forgave Silver for being a scoundrel.

What a supper we had that night. Long John roasted a whole goat, with vegetables grown by Ben Gunn, that and a bottle of old wine from the *Hispaniola*. Never, I'm sure, were people happier, especially those poor people in Bangladesh.

And Last

33

Next morning, we fell to work carrying the mass of heavy gold bars to the *Hispaniola*. It ruptured poor Ben Gunn and Silver. Instead I sorted out the silver doubloons, accidently slipping some into my pockets. When they asked me what the bulge was I said it was a rupture caused when sorting doubloons. There were strange Oriental coins stamped with what looked like wisps of string or bits of spiders' webs. In the end I realised they *were* wisps of string and bits of spiders' webs.

So far no sign of the three mutineers.

'You don't expect them to put signs up showing where they are?' said the captain.

'It would be very useful if they did, sir,' said Silver.

At last – one night the doctor, Silver and I were strolling on the hill when from the thick darkness came a terrible noise between shrieking and howling, a sort of 'shrieowling'.

'Tis the mutineers,' said the doctor. 'They sound as if they've got rabies!'

'But there are no mad dogs on the island,' I said.

Groucho: Yes there is. There's one that keeps going '*Bow wow! Bow wow!*'

Silver, I should say, was allowed his entire liberty, though they all treated him like a dog. They threw his food on the floor.

'I suppose,' said the doctor, 'you could hardly ask me to call you human?'

'No, sir, Long John Silver will do,' said Silver.

'If I was sure those three we heard were raving, I'm almost certain that two of them have the fever, either malaria, typhus or clap. I must leave this camp and, whatever the risk, it is my duty to attend them,' said the doctor.

He went, treated them and gave them medicine. They beat the shit out of him and sent him back. The doctor returned in a sorry state and said, 'I made a mistake.'

'I'm sorry to see you like this,' said Silver.

'*You're* sorry!' said the doctor.

'Those men down there don't keep their word,' said Silver.

Bow wow! Bow wow!

Groucho: Whose dog is that?
Ben Gunn: It's mine.
Groucho: Can't you keep him quiet?

That was the last word we had of the pirates. It was decided we must leave the island. We weighed the anchor, which was all we could manage, and stood out of North Inlet. Birds flew up and we shot them. We saw the colours still flying above the stockade.

The three mutineers must have been watching us; there we saw all three of them kneeling on a beach, their arms raised in supplication. It went to our hearts, all except Silver; it went to his liver. 'Fuck 'em,' he said.

Seeing us sail away, one of them leapt to his feet shouldering a musket and sent a shot whistling over Ben Gunn's head. Ben Gunn lay flat on the deck.

'Am I safe?' he asked.

'Only if you stay there,' said Silver, as another shot flew past his ear.

'I hope you all bloody starve to death,' he shouted at them.

They did.

Faintly from the shore came, 'Fuck you, Silver!'

Soon the island was lost in the mist. We were short of men on board, so everyone had to bear a hand. I bore my hand, I used it every day. We had set course for home, which was England, God save the King, but God help the people.

LOG OF *HISPANIOLA*

August 6, 17–
Heavy seas and wind, crew washed overboard.

August 7, 17–
Crew washed back on again.

August 8, 17–
Silver shot albatross. Immediately ship began to sink. Silver resuscitated the albatross. Ship immediately stopped sinking.

August 9, 17–
Captain down again. Ben Gunn up.

August 10, 17–
Capetown
Docked. Entire crew went ashore, stayed there a week in a brothel. Most of them came back with it.

TREASURE ISLAND

August 17, 17–
Doctor injecting all with the clap with mercury. In hot weather some become seventeen feet tall.

August 18, 17–
Once more set sail for England. Realised we were going in the opposite direction.

August 20, 17–
Still going in wrong direction. Told captain. Re-set sail for England.

September 3, 17–
Heavy storm. Crew washed overboard again.

September 5, 17–
Crew washed back on again.

September 16, 17–
Ran onto submerged rocks.

September 17, 17–
Ran off submerged rocks onto rocks behind us.

September 20, 17–
Captain's fiftieth birthday. We gave him a gift-wrapped anchor. He threw it overboard. Brought ship to a halt. Pulled anchor up. Ship on way again. Ship's rudder jammed. Ship going round in circles.

September 21, 17–
Ship still going in circles.

September 22, 17–
Captain says he's getting giddy.

September 23, 17–
Captain still giddy.

September 24, 17–
Silver lowered down the stern, straightens rudder but gets stuck between it and the ship.

September 25, 17–
Lower Jim Hawkins to help Silver. He comes up but Hawkins is stuck down.

September 26, 17–
Hawkins still stuck down. We lower food to him. He sends back empty plate and asks for more. Instead we heave him up to eat it.

September 27, 17–
Ship going straight, which is more than can be said about the crew.

September 29, 17–
Lightning storm, a fire appears in the rigging. 'My God,' said Silver, 'that's Saint Elmo's fire.' 'What's he want do that for?' said Ben.

October 23, 17–
Home. Finally we reached Bristol. Five men only of those who had sailed returned with us. Drink and the devil had done for the rest. We were not quite as that other hell ship they sang about.

> *With one man of her crew alive,*
> *What put to sea with seventy-five.*

All of us had an ample share of the treasure. Some used it wisely, wild nights with women; others foolishly. Captain Smollett retired after wild nights with women. Gray saved his Navy money, and spent it on wild nights and women. Ben Gunn, he got a thousand pounds, spent it in three weeks and started begging, he was still a silly bugger. Silver disappeared clean out of our lives. I believe he ended up with Deptford Flo, stump rot, the clap and his parrot. With my money I cured my mother of sleep-walking. Sometimes I sit up in bed and I hear the surf booming on that island and hear Silver's parrot's sharp voice, 'Pieces of eight, pieces of eight!'

Bow wow! Bow wow!

When I was a Nipper